The Jesus Wars

Lorna Wood

ISBN-13: 979-8-7097-4567-4

DEDICATION

To Don, with much love.

CONTENTS

I THE POWER TOOLS OF JESUS

Easter Sunday, 2002, was just like any Easter Sunday as far back as anyone in Jubilee, Georgia, could remember. At the time, no one realized what a powder keg Jubilee had become, what with 9/11, the invasion of Afghanistan, and the dispute over the Georgia state flag. But over at First Baptist Church of Jubilee Pastor Hunter Long's sermon on the "Power of Jesus" was about to touch off a conflict destined to shake the town to its very foundation.

A good while ago, Pastor Long had pulled himself out of Megiddo, Georgia (population 623), by the straps of his overalls, and taking heed of Lot's wife, he had only looked up and ahead ever since. Now, with his dark eyes sparkling with zeal, his aquiline nose, and his shiny bald dome rising to a seemingly impossible height between two symmetrical patches of salt-and-pepper hair, he perched serenely atop a hierarchy of support personnel that went from security, janitorial, nursery, and clerical staff all the way up to assistant ministers.

True, his resemblance to a raptor gave many pause, and some of his flock were convinced he was perpetually hovering, ready to swoop down on stray souls and gather them to God in his talons. But this notion of his character was belied by his voice, which was as soft and soothing as a caress. Even the most impassioned flights of his sermons sounded to his flock like the soughings of a great sea, sighing over their many sins and longing to transport them to a better place.

His hands, too, though large and long-fingered, had a surprising grace. He always kept them impeccably manicured, as if in constant watchfulness against the dirt that had once resisted even the harshest scrubbings of his mamma's lye soap. And though he might clasp his parishioners with paternal firmness or heartily clap a good old friend on the back, when he illustrated the simplicity of the spiritual path laid out for us, the white cleanness of his hands fluttered like doves' wings, making feathery tracings though the air.

For all that, he retained a workingman's simplicity and enjoyed bringing earthy, everyday life into his sermons. Everyone remembered the time he brought his dog in to illustrate faithfulness, so everyone knew there'd be some kind of special something to help bring the sermon home for Easter. And everyone was excited to find out what it would be.

#

Already an imposing building when erected in 1859, the First Baptist Church of Jubilee had been renovated and considerably enlarged over the years. So just before 10 a.m. on that Easter, a number of people climbed the steep steps to its grandly pillared façade on Second Avenue, right across from the Jubilee Town Square, while others entered via the new Family Life Wing on Blossom Street, which had a wheelchair ramp, or through the offices, one block north, on Church Street.

Once inside, the large, friendly congregation milled about gregariously until a little after ten, when even loiterers and latecomers had found seats in the sanctuary, and the service began. First came stirring choral music and welcoming prayers, punctuated by baptisms of various new and recommitted congregants in a cross-shaped blue plastic font with a plexiglass panel for viewing the actual moment of immersion. Then, after another musical interlude, during which Pastor Long quick-changed into dry clothes, he strode out onto the wide, low stage in his shirtsleeves, carrying a large sawhorse in one hand and a gleaming saw in the other. Behind him came his wife Melanie, carrying another sawhorse. An anticipatory murmur went through the crowd.

Without immediately acknowledging them, Pastor Long picked up a plank from in front of the altar, set it across the sawhorses, and began to saw. The regular sound of it was soothing at first, but then nerve wracking. It seemed to stretch time in the big, quiet sanctuary, like a clock ticking away a long afternoon. But just as people were beginning to give each other questioning glances, the pastor pulled out an enormous red paisley bandanna, shook it out to its full, gaudy length, and proceeded to wipe his brow before going back to sawing. As the laughter died away, the room grew electric with suppressed anticipation. Surely that bandanna presaged some remarkable entertainment.

Still sawing, Pastor Long began to talk. "This sure is hard work." More sawing, then, "I'm starting to wish I hadn't promised Melanie that new house" (a laugh from the audience, and he went back to sawing). "I mean, if I can't even get this one little old cross done for Easter, I honestly don't know how I'm gonna finish building her that house by Mother's Day" (more sawing).

Suddenly he laid the saw down and turned to face his audience. "But enough about me and my problems. We're here to talk about Jesus our Lord's resurrection!" He stretched out his arms, and his dark eyes gleamed with fire, while his soft voice yearned for the shining clouds of heaven. Briefly he told the story of the empty tomb, the road to Emmaus, the appearance to the Apostles, all the while striding up and down in front of the sawhorse.

Finally, he confronted them. "Now friends, I believe most of you know this story. You know how it illustrates the incredible *power* of Jesus to overcome death. You may even be saying, 'But Pastor Long, of course I believe in the power of Jesus; I believe He rose from the dead on the third day to sit at the right hand of the Father—the Bible tells me all that, and I believe it.'

"I hope most of you will even say, 'Yes, and I believe the power of Jesus *saved* me so that if I die tomorrow—' and friends, none of us know when our time will be—'if I die tomorrow I *know* I'm goin' to heaven.'

"But I suspect a few of you—maybe even more than a few—are wondering, 'Where can I find the power of Jesus in my life today?'

"My friends, I'm gonna tell you, and it's very simple. The power of Jesus is Everywhere, and it'll help you do Everything. Anything you put your mind to, it'll get easier with Jesus. That's His promise to you, my friends."

He went around behind the sawhorse and began to saw again. "So, for instance, maybe you feel—I don't know—stuck in a groove, just goin' back and forth, nothing much to show for it—sure would be nice. . . ." The pastor's soft voice died away as he looked off toward the pulpit.

Suddenly he did a double take and put down the saw again. "Wait a minute . . . " He bent down behind the pulpit, emerging a moment later with a six-inch circular saw in one hand and a drill in the other. "Lookee here!" He pointed the drill at the congregation. *Bzzzh!* He brandished the saw in the other hand. *Whirrr!* In the front rows, some of the more nervous members of the congregation flinched. "Change is a-comin', my friends."

He applied the saw to the plank. In an instant, the wood lay in two pieces. Pastor Long picked up the longer board, laid it over the sawhorses, and commenced to screw the smaller board across it. "You see, tryin' to accomplish anything without Jesus is just like me sawin' away at that board for hours on end. You're just not gonna get very far." (*Bzzht, bzzht, bzzht, bzzht!* went the drill, making four pilot holes.)

"But when you got the power of Jesus, friends," said the minister, contemplatively changing his drill bit, "well, it all gets easier, don't it?" He got four screws out of his pocket. *Bzzht, bzzht, bzzht, bzzht!* In they went.

"Don't get me wrong, you still got to build." He turned to accept a banner of white cloth from his wife, who had come back up from the front row. "The love of a good woman don't hurt, neither," he said, with a fatherly wink.

"But if you want to do something great," he continued, lovingly draping the cloth over his creation, "take it from me, you got to turn on the power of Jesus in your life." He picked up the drill and the saw and gave Melanie a nod.

They stepped from behind the sawhorse. Melanie raised the cross high, so the ends of its banner floated and settled. Pastor Long held up the tools like a cowboy with two six-shooters. "My friends, when you get the power of Jesus in your life, suddenly you can build a fulfilling career" (*Whirr!*), "truly loving relationships" (*Bzzzh!*), "stronger families" (*Whirr!*). "At the end of the day you can step back and be proud of what you've done because it wasn't just you that did it. No! You had the power of Jesus working *through* you, my friends." He gave a final parting *Bzzzzh!* before laying down the tools.

The crowd was so excited that they could hardly pay attention while Pastor Long went on to explain how prayer was the way to turn on Jesus power in their lives. Indeed, the power-drill sermon made a long-lasting impression, entering into the everyday life of the town. Little boys chased each other or their favorite little girls around on the playground, wielding imaginary "Jesus guns" and making their own *Bzzh!* sounds. Men reminded their wives and girlfriends of their sovereignty, either by warning them against interrupting the "Lord's work" going on in their hobby rooms, garages and backyards, or, in rarer cases, presenting tokens of their Jesus power—little gifts or items crossed off their honey-do lists. Less fortunate or handy men went out and bought power tools for the first time in their lives, as did a few of the more enterprising or frustrated women. At least one lasting match arose from a chance meeting in Jubilee Hardware—which only enhanced the craze.

In no time Methodists and even Presbyterians were in on the Jesus Power phenomenon. Several attended First Baptist for the first time over the ensuing Sundays, seeking inspiration, as they put it, though secretly hoping for another spectacle. A few discovered a new church home (Clayton Briggs, the proprietor of Jubilee Hardware and a lifelong Methodist, converted on the spot). That spring, as Jubilee United Methodist searched for a new music minister, there was a distinct pressure to get someone who could really put on a show.

II JUBILEE AND THE FLAG CONTROVERSY

For almost a century and a half—ever since their founding, following the incorporation of Jubilee in 1829—the First Baptist Church of Jubilee and Jubilee United Methodist had been harmonious neighbors of equal standing in the community. Both church buildings served as makeshift hospitals during the Civil War, and both stood shoulder to shoulder against integration for as long as possible, although the Methodists were more moderate in expressing their views. It therefore startled many when the Methodists entered into open rivalry with their neighbor. Before blaming JUMC's ministerial staff for trying to compete with Pastor Long, however, we must recall that they were also responding more generally to the community's need for healing after 9/11 and the troubling effects of the state flag controversy. Fanned by the media, this dispute had caused a recent flare-up of racial tensions in Jubilee.

Most people believed that the 1956 flag repealed in January of 2001 had "always" been the flag, and anyway its stars and bars were just a symbol of Southern heritage and the right to self-determination—and what could be more American than that? This Rebel spirit was supported by the national controversy raging concurrently over a legal challenge to the phrase "under God" (also inserted in the '50s) in the Pledge of Allegiance—everyone agreed *that* case was just an attack on patriotic values, plain and simple—and by outrage over the 9/11 attacks. All were eager to show their patriotic Christianity by flying every flag pertinent to their heritage as often and prominently as possible.

In accord with these sentiments, the Jubilee city fathers (Johnny Abbott, the African American representative for Ward 4, dissenting) voted soon after the repeal to adopt the discarded state flag as the municipal emblem of Jubilee, and it now flew not only from the façade of the courthouse and in front of other official buildings, but also, on Confederate holidays, from the porches of many private dwellings. But residents of Jubilee from the other side of the tracks in Ward 4 (who happened to be African American) were affronted at the prospect of a relic of slavery being so ubiquitously flaunted on Martin Luther King Day, which was celebrated on the same day as the municipal holiday of Robert E. Lee's Birthday. With the help of Johnny Abbott and his energetic mother, Althea Abbott Henderson, they organized and obtained permits for a monumental Martin Luther King Day parade that promised to tie up traffic around the town square for the entire morning.

Not backing down, the city council members who happened to be white collaborated with Confederate-friendly organizations to organize their own parade. Jubilee Christian Academy (founded 1965), frat boys from the Southern Heritage Society of nearby Northwest Georgia State University, and the Jubilee chapters of the Georgia Reenactors Association and the Daughters of the Confederacy all pitched in. In addition to promising traffic tie-ups for the rest of the day, this plan drew national media attention.

Desperate for fodder, Botoxified talking heads descended on Jubilee, clogging the motels and at once thrilling and annoying the startled populace. Althea Henderson was much sought after, especially once Johnny, never shy of the limelight, shared her storied history. Beginning as a sharecropper's daughter (one of nine children), she had participated in the Civil Rights Movement, where she had met Dr. King and been scarred by fire hoses. Moreover, she had, besides Johnny, another son, a national hero who was suffering from cancer linked to his heroic role as a first responder in 9/11. Topping it all off was her rise to riches upon her second marriage to Isaiah "Izzy" Henderson of Henderson's BBQ. The heads fell over one another to get to this dignified woman, known for her elegant hats and iron discipline. This publicity was such that later it was credited with laying the foundation for Johnny Abbott's congressional career.

The reenactors were filmed drilling and telling the story of how the Yankee hordes (really a small reconnaissance party) were turned back at Jubilee Creek, which, after years of defilement by the Braxton Mills textile manufacturers, was now being cleaned up by the Reenactors' Association, the Braxton Foundation, and various organizations dedicated to restoring Civil War battlefields (Braxton Mills having moved its last finishing plant to China five years ago). Someone was sold footage of the acrimonious Jubilee Town Council meeting in which the city flag had been adopted over the vociferous protests of Johnny Abbott and Ward 4 residents (a few blows had been exchanged afterwards by hotheaded adherents of both sides). On a tip, someone else ran Fred Hollifield, Senior Minister of Jubilee United Methodist, to earth and got his footage and recollections of the high school's first integrated "alternative" prom in 1976, which he had hosted at JUMC (the high school held out until 1989, when only a handful of students still supported the segregated version). Other enterprising journalists found footage on the Internet of Omega Phi Epsilon's Southern Heritage Parade (discontinued by NWGSU in 1995), which featured manacled students in blackface, and Fox News dug up unrelated footage of the college's African American dance crew stepping enthusiastically to a Public Enemy rap promoting violence against the Establishment.

The prominent citizens of Jubilee found themselves bustled hither and yon, but the heads were not about to let the fires they had started be easily smothered. In the current contentious atmosphere, a bloodthirsty CNN reporter asked breathlessly, could the Klan resist an opportunity to rear its hooded head?

Now the Klan had not been publicly active in the area around Jubilee since they protested the alternative prom in 1976 by burning a cross on Fred Hollifield's front lawn and spray painting "nigger lover" across the side of the church next to the parking lot. The very existence of the Klan was generally regarded as embarrassing, to say the least. The local organization had not recruited many new members lately, and its old-school leaders, like Clint Farrow, who lived reclusively on a small antebellum plantation outside of town, did not cotton to the skin-headed, spider-tattooed jailbirds who did show up now and then.

The national Klan responded to the media's invitation, however. The Imperial Wizard in Ohio organized a "Freedom Bus" to come down and participate in the Robert E. Lee parade. The heads were in ecstasies. Would there be violence? United in obstructing the paperwork for the Freedom Bus, the city fathers hired the best lawyer in town to find a reason to prevent the Klan's participation, but fortunately the situation was resolved when the Wizard was arrested on outstanding warrants.

That was about as far as it all went. Both parades were held without violence. The African Americans went home after theirs satisfied at having yet again aspersed the stone of racism, which would one day be worn away. Likewise, in the late afternoon the whites went home satisfied at having once again defended their enduring traditions. Only the heads were disappointed. But despite the general satisfaction and the economic windfall from weeks of media attention, the town and surrounding area were left licking all the old wounds the episode had painfully reopened, and it was only natural that one or the other of its two most prominent churches should attempt to dress them.

III ANSWERED PRAYERS

The most promising candidate for JUMC's vacant music position was Braden Miller, a wiry young man with tastefully highlighted blond hair that kept falling into his eyes and a deceptive air of diffidence when you first spoke with him. He had always known he was different, and not just because his mother told everyone so. Fortunately, in the small town of Noble, Alabama, manners were still important: niceness was valued, bullying almost unknown. This, coupled with his mother's pride in his musical and academic achievements, meant Braden's self-esteem had never been in serious jeopardy as he grew up. Still, he felt uncomfortable often enough that show choir came as a welcome relief.

He knew immediately that this was what he wanted to do for the rest of his life, only he wanted to do it for Jesus. He knew this was possible from watching the Crystal Cathedral's *Hour of Power* and from shows he had seen with his cousins in Nashville. His girlfriend, Brenda Doughty, whom he met around this time while helping her with a show choir routine, encouraged him in his dreams, shared his faith, and admired his sexual restraint.

You could have knocked him over with a feather when his church's music director seduced him one night after choir practice, inspiring him with confused feelings of delight and self-loathing, affection and fear, pride and overwhelming embarrassment. "Don't tell Joan, she's a wonderful woman," Mr. Garrett had whispered, almost pushing him out the door—and the next day, wanting to make it all better, Braden had given Brenda his class ring to wear on a chain around her neck.

From then on, he fell into a pattern. He conscientiously fulfilled his duties: schoolwork, church (choir continued, though he avoided eye contact when he encountered the Garretts socially), helping his single mom, paying attention to Brenda. In show choir he shone brightest, and already in his junior year he was helping with choreography, choice of repertoire, costumes, tour organization and planning.

And then there was his other self, which he imagined as a beautiful, poisonous flower unfolding in the darkness, though in reality the blooming occurred mainly under the fluorescent lights of the Atlas Gym, where he at first got a job in maintenance—cleaning, setting up, putting away—but was eventually promoted to trainer, and where he soon learned that he and Mr. Garrett were not the only people in Noble with a secret.

College changed little. Braden continued at once conscientious and traitorous to all he believed. But by this time he was too deeply committed to his mother, to Brenda, and to his faith to come out, and he was not at all sure that the openly gay lifestyle was morally superior to the compartmentalized one he had constructed for himself.

He only knew—after many prayers and failed attempts—that he would not be able to stop, to leave the secret, sweaty joy of strong, hard male bodies clinging together. Or even slightly gone-to-seed male bodies like Mr. Garrett's. Braden was never overly particular—the details of the encounter did not matter as much as the shared acknowledgement he perpetually craved.

With a masters in choral conducting from Samford University forthcoming, Braden interviewed for jobs. Some ministers seemed a mismatch—their stiffness reminding him of his old feelings of discomfort back in Noble. Others clearly did not share his passion for putting on a show or could not come up with the requisite budget.

And so it was that on a pleasant day in May 2002, Braden arrived in Jubilee in time for lunch. He parked on First Avenue by the town square and, following some information derived from the Internet, walked a block over to Henderson's BBQ, where he had a delicious half rack of ribs with Henderson's secret sauce and, looking around at the clientele, felt right at home. There was a pleasant clatter of conversation and silverware from the business people and shoppers that was festive and in keeping with the deliciousness of the fare, and the line of working people picking up orders at the counter kept up an amusingly earthy stream of pleasantries among themselves and with the young African American woman behind the register.

Returning to the square, still with time on his hands, Braden inspected the heroic figure on the Confederate War Memorial in its center and then walked over to a plaque erected by the Daughters of the Confederacy on the corner of Blossom and Second Avenue, catty-corner to the First Baptist church. This informed passersby of the heroic exploits of Jubilee's Petticoat Army, which on this very spot, then called "Jubilee Junction," bravely repelled a marauding party of Yankees in October 1864.

Intrigued by the massive neoclassicism of First Baptist, Braden continued north on Second, pausing to read the marquee in front of the church ("God vs. the ACLU") and to admire its imposing front entrance. Then, noticing the time, he returned to Blossom Street and walked past His Word Christian Bookstore, Sam's Pizza, and Jubilee Hardware. Crossing First Avenue on the other side of the square, he arrived at Jubilee United Methodist.

Here Braden again stopped to admire the architecture. Rebuilt in 1956 after a termite infestation destroyed the original structure, JUMC conveys everything solid and reassuring about that era. Set back from the street, so that one approaches it via a cement path shaded by gracious magnolias, it is balanced and neoclassical, but not in the massive manner of First Baptist. Its bricks are not painted white (recalling marble's adamantine purity), but radiate a warm red glow, and though it has a grandly pillared portico and three white doors, the central one being double, there are only three low, broad cement steps leading up to it. Receding from the central building on one side and occupying an entire block of First Avenue is the John and Sarah Grantwell Education Wing, housing a nursery school, kindergarten, and mother's day out program, as well as church offices. On the other side, occupying only the narrow Church Drive off Blossom Street, is the Evan and Marie Butler Fellowship Wing, housing community and charitable outreach endeavors, as well as a smaller chapel for more intimate worship experiences. Though bigger than Braden's church back in Noble, JUMC was similar enough to give him a feeling of home.

Locating the Grantwell Wing as instructed, Braden was trying various doors when he was hailed from above. "Don't worry, Mr. Miller—you've come to the right place!"

Looking up, he saw the head and broad shoulders of an elderly man protruding from a second-story window. "I'm Reverend Hollifield. I've sent my associate, Cyrus Buell, down to open up for you."

"Thank you," Braden yelled up, as the head and shoulders disappeared.

In a moment, Cyrus let Braden in and introduced himself, shaking hands. They ascended the stairs to a small conference room, where, sitting around a dark wooden table, were Reverend Hollifield, Youth Minister Craig Wright, and Jim Engels, the organist. (Marian Hollifield, the reverend's wife and Director of the Sunday School, was unable to attend). During the ensuing interview, Braden began to form impressions of his future colleagues.

Reverend Hollifield was humble but dignified. In his early seventies, he had kindly blue eyes that often seemed focused on matters above and beyond those at hand and scrubby white hair that stuck up in the back no matter how many times he smoothed it. Possessed of a simple, childlike faith, the old man often seemed only a pair of wings shy of being an angel. Only later did Braden learn of the reverend's dramatic preaching style—his singsong delivery, illustrated with grandiose gestures. In the interview he was all genial admiration when he grasped Braden's vision for JUMC's music program, and best of all he seemed completely innocent of gaydar.

Cyrus Buell, the associate minister, was plump, with wide round eyes set in a smooth face. Like his superior, Cyrus was humble, earnest, and unassuming, but if Fred Hollifield conveyed awe and wistful wonder at the mysteries of the divine, Cyrus never went beyond bewilderment. He spoke slowly and seriously, and only when absolutely necessary.

Craig Wright, on the other hand, was energetic, with closely cropped sandy hair and an athletic build. He gave Braden the impression of a man who harbored strong convictions and didn't like to be crossed, but in the interview this was entirely to Braden's advantage, as Craig was the most forthcoming about the need for healing after the media's violation of Jubilee during the flag controversy, as well as about the gimmicks employed by "that other church across the way," as he darkly characterized FBCJ.

Finally, there was Jim Engels, a tall, powerfully built man in his early forties with dark brown, wavy hair streaked with gray and a beard. He had a rich, fruity baritone but said little during the interview, merely sitting back deliberatively, arms and legs crossed. "Is he or isn't he?" Braden asked himself, surreptitiously observing the organist and wondering if it was his imagination or if Jim really was checking him out in return.

Only afterward, when everything had gone well, with Reverend Hollifield captivated by Braden's description of a possible Fourth of July program and the lesser ministers falling into line behind him, did Braden feel sure, though really, he could count the number of straight male organists he had known on the fingers of one hand. When everyone had shaken Braden's hand again, and the Reverend Hollifield had promised him warmly that he would be hearing from them soon, Jim lingered behind as the others left.

He put a fatherly arm around Braden's shoulders. "Don't fret now. It's in the bag," he said confidentially, with a little squeeze. "I knew as soon as you walked in that you were just the man for the job. You got Vision."

"Why thank you," said Braden, tossing his hair. "We're gonna shake things up around here."

"I know you will," Jim said, and he gave a little wink as he let Braden go.

IV BATTLE PLANS AND RECRUITMENT

Braden laid out the program for JUMC's First Annual Fourth of July Celebration in three parts. In "Heritage of Freedom," America's conception as a new land of opportunity and religious freedom would be celebrated in words, hymns, and slides, culminating in excerpts from Martin Luther King's speeches and a sad spiritual. Part two, "Sweet Land of Liberty," would pay tribute to Jubilee's heritage, celebrating Celtic immigrants with a Riverdance version of "The Lord of the Dance" sung by the Youth Choir, commemorating the Confederacy with a reenactment of the Petticoat Army's heroic defense of Jubilee (finished off with an arrangement of "Dixie" tastefully combined with Rossini's *William Tell* overture), and, for the first-half finale, celebrating the town's African roots with "The Circle of Life" from Disney's *The Lion King.* After an intermission, "Defense of Freedom" would patriotically support our nation's military with the Pledge of Allegiance, "The Battle Hymn of the Republic" (carefully introduced), a medley of the songs of each branch of the Armed Forces, accompanied by a color guard and memorial wreath procession, and a rousing rendition of "The Star Spangled Banner" (during which the banner itself would rise above the altar), with confetti cannon fired at the finish.

He pulled out all the stops to make his vision a reality. With the choir he was a fireball of energy. For the story of the Pilgrims—beginning with a reading (in darkness save for a single spotlight, and accompanied by organ music), through the solemn processional ("Lead Us, Heavenly Father"), to the stirring finale ("Holy, Holy, Holy"), Braden made his choir relive the persecution and sufferings of those early immigrants over and over again.

But these were his people, and he knew they needed more, a living, breathing tug on their heartstrings to inspire them. So after doing the dramatic reading himself while he reconnoitered, he finally chose Marvin Patterson, the recently widowed principal of Jubilee's Munroe High School, who was active in community theater and equipped with a deep, if erratic, bass voice and the lugubrious demeanor of a Bassett Hound.

"Marvin," Braden said softly, taking him aside after practice one evening early on. "Things are pretty dark right now, aren't they?" Braden would have put an arm around his shoulders, but he couldn't quite reach, so he put it just below, around his arms. "Come on in my office. Let's have a talk."

Marvin nodded dumbly and shuffled down the hall with the music minister. As Braden unlocked the door to his office, the big man looked around helplessly at the emptying hallway.

"G'night, Marvin!" sang out twice-divorced Rita Hill, managing to inject a note of concern into her hopefulness.

Marvin half waved a heavy hand in her direction, shambled into the office, and fell heavily into a chair. "You know," he said, looking vacantly around at the posters of inspirational musical ensembles Braden had hung on the walls, "I still can't help feelin' Linda's going to come up behind me any minute and start tellin' me what to do, just like she used to."

"I wish I could have known her," Braden said. "But Marvin, don't you think you may feel that way because she *is* here, looking down on you all the time?"

Marvin looked at the posters again, as if hoping to see his wife's face in them. "I wanna believe that. I truly do," he said.

Braden pressed his advantage. "And what would she say, do you think, if she were right here now, speaking to you like I am now. What would she tell you?"

A wistful smile spread slowly over his face. "Probly tell me to pull my socks up, I guess," he said ruefully.

Braden allowed himself a smile. ""She sounds like my kinda woman, Marvin."

The man grinned shyly back. "She was one in a million. Yes she was."

"Marvin," Braden said, getting to his feet abruptly, as if he had just made the decision. "Tell you what we're gonna do."

Marvin raised his head, startled and brought to bay.

"We're gonna help you pull your socks up, Marvin, just like Linda would want you to." Braden held up a hand to stave off interruption. "But more than that, I pledge to you here and now—and you can take it to the bank—this entire choir is gonna be a light to you in the darkness"—his hand became a beacon—"until you can shine on your own again. OK?"

Put like that, the task of dramatic reading was too great a favor to turn down. When Braden presented him at the choir rehearsal as an inspiration for all those wandering in loss and uncertainty, like the Pilgrims themselves, Marvin looked modestly down at his shoes but did not demur. This time they sang "Lead Us Heavenly Father" directly to Marvin, with true feeling. Rita Hill and the altos were especially affecting in the first verse, when Braden asked them to sing it on their own.

This was fortunate because Rita owned and ran Jubilee's Superstarz! Academy, featuring ballet, tap, and Irish dancing, voice, keyboard, and guitar lessons, as well as pageant coaching for all ages. Softened up by Braden's sincere compliments and the "marvelous way," as she told him, he had helped Marvin, Rita readily agreed to bring a troop of her Irish dancers for the "Lord of the Dance"/Riverdance number.

#

For the spiritual and the "beauty of the lilies" verse of "The Battle Hymn of the Republic," Braden knew exactly who he wanted: Izzy Henderson's daughter, Yolanda Henderson Tibbets. Busy as she was overseeing the expansion of Henderson's BBQ across the length and breadth of Georgia, Yolanda largely confined her vocal performances in Jubilee to Mt. Zion Missionary Baptist Church, but through his liaison with Alessandro Trentini, the strings teacher at NWGSU, whom he encountered haphazardly at the college's athletic facilities, Braden learned that her voice, with its enormous and powerful range, was in demand as far away as Atlanta.

As soon as he was hired in mid-May, Braden began to eat at Henderson's BBQ on a regular basis. Whenever Yolanda was on hand supervising, which was often, Braden ladled on the charm. He complimented her on her clothes, especially if they were new or glamorous. He brought in Brenda and his mother and introduced them in courtly fashion. He wheedled her for her father's secret sauce recipe, and he persuaded Reverend Hollifield to contract Henderson's to cater the local Ministers' Conference when it was JUMC's turn to host it.

In early June, Braden could not wait any longer. He made an appointment to see Mrs. Tibbets in her office at the back of the restaurant and was ushered inside.

Fortunately, Yolanda was dressed to the nines in a lilac silk suit and a purple hat with a red silk flower on it. Braden clutched at his polo shirt over where his heart was. "Mizz Tibbets! *Where* did you get that *hat*!" He froze for a moment in beseeching admiration.

"Oh now, Mr. Miller," she said reprovingly. "You shouldn't go around flirting with a fat old woman like me. But if you must know, Althea made it for me. You really like it?" She raised a hand to the flower and smiled coquettishly.

"Honey, you're a *vision*," Braden said. "And Mizz Henderson is a genius." He sank into the chair opposite her and contemplated her loveliness.

Yolanda smiled again. "Oh, get along with you now, Mr. Miller," she said. "I know you didn't come just to look at my hat."

"No, Mizz Tibbets, though missing it would have been a tragedy. I'm here to offer you a business proposition."

"Hmmph. I mighta known you was just tryin' to soften up this old lady here," said Mrs. Tibbets. She sat down behind her desk to pull up her calendar on the computer. "What do you want catered, Mr. Miller?"

"Please, Mizz Tibbets. I hope we know each other better than that by now. Call me Braden."

"If you call me Yolanda," she bridled.

"Yolanda," Braden said, stretching out his arms and the word at the same time. "I'm not gonna lie to you, we both know this community needs some healing after that flag business."

"OK," Yolanda said, her eyes narrowing as they steered into dangerous racial waters.

"We need some food for the soul—some soul food, if you will"—Braden permitted himself this little joke—"and we need leaders of the community to come together and provide it."

"You want Henderson's to hand out *free food*?" Yolanda asked, her eyes flashing.

"Oh no, nothing like that," Braden said, waving both hands to erase the unwelcome specter. "It's just, you see, JUMC is putting on a Fourth of July Celebration, and of course we want the whole community to be a part of it. As a matter of fact—" he had cleared this with Reverend Hollifield weeks ago—"we're prepared to offer you a small honorarium *and* a free, full-page ad for Henderson's Barbecue in the program—this is the weekend *before* the Fourth, mind—in return for—" Braden paused, building the suspense, then leaned forward intimately over the desk. "To tell you the truth, I'm scared you'll turn me down flat."

"Try me, honey," said Yolanda, visibly softened.

Braden took a deep breath and sat up straight in his chair. "Mizz Tibbets—Yolanda—would you do us the honor of singing in our little concert?"

Yolanda's laugh rolled down like mighty waters. "'*Little* concert'! Tell the truth now, Braden. It'll be the biggest thing this town's ever seen. I'll be there with bells on—just *try* and stop me."

She heaved herself up, still shaking with laughter, and offered him a surprisingly dainty hand, which he clasped in both his own with courtly gratitude. She was in the bag.

V POOR MISS SARAH JO, BLESS HER HEART, AND THE BELL CHOIR

There were only a few personnel problems left to be solved. May Ewing, who was a large, aggressively bossy woman completely at odds with her pastoral name, was not best pleased to learn that Yolanda Tibbets, not even a church member, had been handed the kind of plum solos previously reserved for May herself. Smelling blood, the soprano section, over whom she had tyrannized for many a long year, came to Braden in a body and ever so politely suggested that Mrs. Yarnell, the new music teacher over at the junior high, be put in charge of them for a change.

At the other end of the spectrum was "poor Miss Sarah Jo, bless her heart," as she was generally called. Under her hesitant direction the handbell choir, who were to perform the prelude selections for the concert, had fallen into cacophony, but no one was unfeeling enough to call for her dismissal.

Braden, however, had done his homework thoroughly. Having ascertained from recorded services that Mrs. Ewing's quavering vibrato did not conceal her hit or miss intonation, he had presented a little program at the Jubilee Music Club one Thursday morning and made use of the social hour to inform himself about Sarah Jo Weaver (née Munroe)'s family history.

#

So it was that, soon after his interview with Yolanda, Braden invited himself (poor Sarah Jo could not get about as she used to, bless her heart) to admire Mrs. Weaver's garden and partake of her famous minted peach iced tea.

It was an exceptionally hot day, so after a cursory exposition of her luxuriant gardenias and magnolias, as well as a few bitter aspersions on mimosa and kudzu, Sarah Jo allowed Braden to help her up the steps and into her living room, where Lydie, her maid, served tea and some nuts and chocolates that appeared to date from the same era as the handsome young officer in a Confederate uniform whose full-length portrait hung to the left of the sofa.

This young man, who stood hand on hip with a jaunty, military air, looking almost insolently into the dark, wood-paneled room, was, Braden's research informed him, Captain Septimus Buford Munroe, Sarah Jo's grandfather and a hero of the Skirmish at Jubilee Creek, where he claimed to have lost an eye, though some contended he lost it in a dispute over cards, later.

"Miss Sarah Jo," Braden said, after a sip of tea, "I do believe the rumors are true."

"Oh?" said Sarah Jo, slightly alarmed.

"This *is* the finest iced tea this side of Atlanta." Braden held up his glass and peered into its amber depths.

"Mr. Braden," Sarah Jo said, waving her hand at him and blushing. "That's the heat talking, I'm sure."

"Well in that case the heat has a very discerning palate." He took another, longer sip. It really was refreshing. "But what I actually came for, besides seeing your lovely home—" he peered around as best he could in the gloom—"was to talk about your proud military heritage." He allowed his gaze to rest on Captain Munroe's strong jaw and closely set eyes, imagining his muscular outdoorsman's body under the uniform.

In her armchair, Sarah Jo gave a nervous wriggle. "Oh! And here I was expecting you were going to read me the riot act over the bell choir. But don't worry, Mr. Braden. We'll pull it together all right. Always do. Chocolate?"

Braden leaned forward to forestall her wavering efforts to hand the plate across to him. He got it away from her and put it down, saying, "Oh no. I couldn't, Miss Sarah Jo. Must preserve my girlish figure, you know." He put a hand on his stomach, which seemed always just threatening to bulge these days, despite his efforts at the gym.

Sarah Jo tittered. "Mr. Braden. You *are* a breath of fresh air and no mistake. But tell me, what do you need to know about my family history? I'll be happy to help in any way I can." Her eyes gleamed with unaccustomed keenness, and Braden knew he had hooked her.

"Well, Miss Sarah Jo, I understand you are the direct descendant of Sarah Jane Hyde, grandmother of Captain Munroe and leader of the Petticoat Army in the Incident at Jubilee Junction?"

"I am indeed." Sarah Jo drew herself up a little, turning pink again. "And I'm flattered that you take such an interest. Most young folks today just don't seem to have the time . . . "

"You are so right, Miss Sarah Jo," Braden broke in, setting his iced tea down emphatically on a doily coaster. "It's just a shame, but with your help

I aim to do something about it."

"You do?" quavered Sarah Jo.

"It'll require some sacrifice, mind."

"Sacrifice?"

"Now don't look at me like that, Miss Sarah Jo. Nothing like what your family went through for the Cause. But—I'm just gonna come right out with it: I want JUMC to reenact the Incident as part of our Fourth of July Celebration and I was hoping I might prevail on you to take the part of Mrs. Sarah Jane Hyde."

Sarah Jo gave him a worshipful look and clutched her iced tea convulsively. "Why Mr. Braden. That's a marvelous idea. I could kiss you, if I weren't such an old lady, and you weren't so handsome. But it'll be absolutely no sacrifice a*tall*, I assure you."

Braden shook his head as he bent to pick up his glass. "I'm afraid it will, Miss Sarah Jo. You see, it's a demanding role, and of course we need your historical expertise as well, if we want to do it right. I'm afraid it might mean giving up the bell choir, just for this concert."

"Oh!" Sarah Jo put a hand to her cheek. The iced tea sloshed dangerously in the other. "Yes. Yes, I see what you mean. It certainly *would* be a lot to take on. Still—perhaps I could—" Braden hung fire, but after a moment she set her glass down decisively. "No, no; you're absolutely right, Mr. Braden. It *will* be a lot, and it has to be done right. After all"—she leaned forward—"they're looking down on us—" she gave a sideways glance at the portrait—"and how'm I going to face 'em in the next life if I don't do justice to their memory in this one?"

"Very true," nodded Braden. "You are a true Christian, Miss Sarah Jo."

She beamed at him. "I try to be, Mr. Braden. Of course we all do what we can, I s'pose."

Lydie came in from the kitchen. "More tea, Mr. Miller?" she offered, lifting the pitcher from its large doily.

"Why thank you. Don't mind if I do."

#

Though flinty and difficult, May Ewing was proud of what she thought of as her leadership qualities. The bell choir was a prominent, popular ensemble, and as its director May could expect just as much attention as a soloist, with much more scope for generalship than her position as leader of the sopranos had offered. She accepted the assignment with the proviso that rehearsal time be doubled from once to twice a week, at least until after the concert.

Braden often winced as he passed their rehearsal room over the ensuing weeks and heard May dressing down her troops, and once poor Nel Harrison, always nervous and prone to ringing too early, came flying right into him and sobbed on his shoulder for several minutes before he could even get her a tissue. They did not want to let Braden down, however. No one quit the ensemble outright, and progress could be gauged by the biblical advice May wrote on the board at the end of each week of rehearsals. Week 1: Rebuke is better than the Song of Fools! Week 2: Count! Don't be a Noisy Gong or a Clanging Cymbal! Week 3: Make a Joyful Noise unto the Lord!

VI BATTLE READY

Meanwhile, Braden continued his efforts with the choir. There was diction—getting them to sing "lant off cot-ton," for instance, instead of "lanagodden." There was choreography. "All right, choir, let's start our warm ups. But this time, I want us all to get loose. So when we do our mi-mi-mi-mi's, let's all do a little shimmy. Like this." He bent his knees and then mi-mied up five notes, shaking hips and shoulders, then mi-mied back down, shimmying in the same direction, then straightened, tossing his hair and acknowledging their laughter and applause. "That's the spirit!" he said. "We're gonna get our exercise tonight!" Now come on, put your folders down. Yes, you too Marvin. Hey everyone, look at Lynette. She can shimmy like her sister Kate!" Lynette was Jim Engels' daughter, and her younger sister's name was Katie. She flashed an embarrassed smile at Braden's praise. "That's it," he encouraged, as the move caught on among the women. "Shake it, Rita. I'm gonna put some life in our 'Circle of Life' if it's the last thing I do," and he played the warm-up chord on the piano.

There was no getting them to pick their heads up out of the music, though Braden was successful here and there. For instance, they were able to memorize the first verse and chorus of "Dixie"—most of them knew it already—but Braden knew better than to ask any more of them. Instead he gave the "Injun batter" verse as a solo to Bob Ragsdale, who had a naturally comic air and didn't mind declaring that the cakes made "you fat and a little fatter" as long as his girth was the center of attention. Even so, it was a trial getting them all to rub their stomachs exactly at the "fat or a little fatter" moment.

Braden prayed for patience and gave out only one more verse, a whistle-only solo to handsome contractor Ron Wylie, who would launch into it after some transitional flirtation during which Judy Engels, playing a departing member of the Petticoat Army, was clearly thrilled to smack Ron with her fan and tell him he was "whistlin' Dixie" as far as his interest in *her* was concerned.

#

There were portents the day of the concert. Ron Wylie, out walking his dog early in the morning, swore he saw a bolt of light barreling across the sky in the direction of the quarry operating east of the city limits and just north of the old mills. Nobody knew whether to believe Ron, who was almost as famous for his tall tales as his womanizing, but around ten thirty everyone felt a faint tremor, and at His Word Christian Bookstore Luraleen Whitfield and two customers witnessed an entire tray of Jesus figurines jump from their shelf to certain destruction.

It was quiet after that, however, and anyway the show must go on.

At two fifty-five the Methodist church was full to bursting. While the congregation of First Baptist was larger, JUMC boasted the more influential pillars of the community: the more powerful lawyers and judges, the mayor, the more established doctors, and professional personnel from NWGSU, including the football coach, were all members at this time. But such were the patriotism of Jubilee and the rumors swirling around the Celebration that a broad spectrum of the town had turned out.

There were families with self-conscious young girls swirling and smoothing their summer dresses as they were shooed into the pews, wriggling young boys shined to within an inch of their lives, and unpatriotic babies who had to be carried out by harassed parents. The fathers were earnest young men with hair cut severely short, their keen, light eyes betraying their sense of the heavy responsibility they had taken on. The mothers were equally conscientious. They got their children off to school and camp, cleaned their houses, went to the beauty parlor and the gym. Many were teachers or secretaries or nurses. A few were lawyers or doctors or professors at NWGSU. There were also many older couples walking stiffly together, the men opening doors and ushering the women into pews with courtly gestures. And there were members of the singles group, either small parties of women, or men and women on dates, smiling and laughing with forced vivacity. Here and there were African Americans, either soberly dressed and pushing an elderly white lady's wheelchair or decked out in full holiday finery. Izzy no longer got about much, but Althea was there in a white straw hat with an expansive, undulating brim trimmed in a magnificent cascade of red and blue feathers. In her wake she towed Yolanda's husband, Artie Tibbets, defensive coordinator of the NWGSU Black Bears, and the ubiquitous Johnny Abbott, who paused every few steps to glad-hand the multitude.

Under the atmosphere of camaraderie and suspenseful excitement ran a solemn undercurrent. Children were on their best behavior; holiday greetings were restrained, rather than effusive. Everyone remembered, amid the celebration of American independence, the planes zooming in unbelievably, the smoke billowing, glass and bodies falling. It was reassuring to grasp the thick, glossy programs with the striking picture of a bald eagle on the cover, to sit in fellowship with one's community, to see, while idly flipping through or fanning oneself, the dark, welcoming face of Izzy Henderson on page four, smiling over his spotless white suit and offering a mouthwatering platter of ribs, and then to locate the names of loved ones in the lists of performers in the back.

The orchestra, composed of townspeople and a string quartet recruited and led by Professor Trentini, were making a subdued warm-up racket. Some of the lesser winds, who were high school students, waved to their friends in the pews.

Braden adjusted his red sequined cummerbund and surveyed his choir. Their red, white and blue sequined vests sparkled over their spotless white shirts. Many of the women had added bright red lipstick, American flag earrings, and other holiday touches.

Braden shooed them out so they could enter from the front for the processional. Then he checked the costumes for the Petticoat Army one more time. He felt a heavy hand on his shoulder.

"I'm fixin' to go out now." Braden turned to find Jim Engels, looking polished in his tuxedo, his fine head of hair brushed neatly back.

"Thanks, Jim. Couldn't have done it without you." And Braden found himself momentarily drawn against Jim in a half hug.

It was a reassuring feeling, but short-lived, as Jim pushed him away almost immediately. "All right, all right. I've gotta get out there. Wait—" Jim stopped as he was turning to go. "I'm afraid I've mussed you." Delicately his sausage-like fingers pushed Braden's bangs back into place, and the two men's eyes met in unspoken understanding. Jim's hand slid down, his fingertips grazing Braden's cheek. "There. That's better," Jim said, nodding. "Can't have you looking like something the cat drug in." And with a final nod at the adjustments he had made, Jim was gone.

Braden felt energies moving violently within him. His inner and outer lives converged like tectonic plates as he pictured first Jim tossing him into bed like a plaything, whispering vile obscenities, then the upright, clean-cut community, Brenda and his mom in the front pew, waiting for the love of Jesus to flood forth from his baton into their thirsty souls.

The bell choir had gained in confidence throughout the prelude. Braden heard the last crisp pings of "This land was made for you and me" and quelled his inner conflict. Though his career hung in the balance, he was not the least bit nervous about the performance, only excited, for he knew he had been born to do this. He strode out and mounted the podium as like an athlete claiming Olympic gold.

VII ACTS OF GOD

From the moment the lights dimmed for the prelude—a stirring blend of "America the Beautiful" and "Joyful, Joyful We Adore Thee," played by organ and orchestra—the audience was electrified. After a brief opening prayer, the lights dimmed again, so the choir's candles lit their faces during the processional as if they really were ghostly Pilgrims from the past. Had the carpet not been so thick, you could have heard a pin drop during Marvin's reading. The recorded bits of Martin Luther King's speeches evoked audible sighs and "Amen"'s from the African Americans in the audience, building up the white audience members' suspense and suppressed discomfort like a wave, on the crest of which Yolanda Tibbets rose up, swathed in a midnight-blue spangled gown with diamonds winking at her neck. ("Oh they're real, all right," Luraleen Whitfield assured Sandra and Clayton Briggs. They had all closed up their shops early for the occasion.)

Not a few audience members wiped their eyes as Yolanda sang, first tremulously, then with gathering power, of the chariot "comin' for to carry me home." Marvin Patterson wept openly, finally drawing a large hankie from his pants pocket and blowing a few stentorian blasts—fortunately drowned by the thunderous applause that followed her performance. The African Americans jumped up with cheers of "Hallelujah!" and "Praise Jesus!" and their example gradually inspired the rest, until all who could stand were on their feet.

Yolanda curtsied like royalty. Her second youngest grandchild presented her with a bouquet of roses almost as big as the child herself, and Braden gave her a bouquet of white lilies (later to be used in "The Battle Hymn of the Republic") that he had purchased out of the concert budget.

Gradually the shouts and applause died down, and Braden inwardly blessed his good programming sense as the kids in the Irish dance and the youth choir lined up, not at all abashed at following Yolanda. Cute and lively, they immediately secured the attention of family and friends in the audience. The weakness of the voices and mistakes at the edges of the dance line were lost in the clatter of clogging shoes and the charm of youth.

"Incident at Jubilee Junction" proved more dramatic than anyone could have anticipated. Just as the slide of Jubilee's antebellum Heritage Mansion was projected on the screen behind the altar to the strains of a Virginia reel, there came a bolt of lightning and a clap of thunder that rattled the stained glass windows in their frames. As Ron Wylie, portraying the leader of the marauding Yankees, sauntered into view and began to give his expository speech about preying on the defenseless women and children of Jubilee while their men were at war, the audience was distracted by a renewal of that morning's tremors—but many of them knew the story anyway, and the faint stirrings served mainly to lend verisimilitude to Ron's description of Sherman's far-off artillery.

Sarah Jo was the real surprise. Over Lydie's protestations, she refused to use her walker, but marched straight as an arrow at the head of her troop of belles, carrying her plastic rifle and barking her line—"Clear off, Yankee scum, or we'll fill your yellow hides full of lead!"—so convincingly that several enthusiastic "Yeehaw"'s and a "You tell 'em, Sarah Jo!" could be heard from the audience.

Before the murmurs of surprise had a chance to die down, Judy Engels had rapped Ron smartly with her fan and pranced coquettishly off the stage, and Ron had launched into his "Whistlin' Dixie" solo. The audience, primed by the skit and divided along gender preference lines between susceptibility to and envy of Ron's charms, nearly drowned him out with cheering (African Americans excepted). They calmed down, however, in time to be bewildered by the orchestra's interjection of the *Lone Ranger* theme (*William Tell* overture), intrigued when it cadenced in "Look away, Dixieland," amused by Bob Ragsdale on the "Injun batter" verse, and thrilled when it all wound up with the final chorus.

Indeed, such whooping and hollering filled the sanctuary that no one even noticed when another bolt of lightning struck nearby, and faintly renewed seismic activity was indistinguishable from vibrations caused by stomping feet. Only the African Americans remained seated, applauding politely. Always the politician, Johnny Abbott did attempt to get up but was pulled back down by Althea, who gave him one of her looks.

The effects of the storm and the fault lines were sadly apparent, however, when "Circle of Life" began and the electricity failed. While Yolanda's solos on the verses rang out clear and true, the weakness of the choir's voices became painfully apparent as they tried to compete with the orchestra without the aid of microphones. The men, already fewer in number than the women, especially faltered when they had to shake their maracas, as the effort required to stay on the beat distracted them. Rita manipulated the rain stick expertly enough, but it could hardly compete with the tempest outside, and its bright colors did not penetrate the gloom. Everyone shimmied on cue, but without illumination the sequined vests did not sparkle, and the effect was underwhelming. Likewise the lion and lamb kites swooped around from fishing poles over the circle the choir had formed failed to garner admiring gasps from the audience, who had just managed to make out what they were as the song ended and Braden, fighting tears, announced intermission.

#

He tried to hole up in his office, but to his surprise an unending stream of well-wishers stopped by to congratulate him. Several of them said the Celebration was "the biggest thing this sleepy little town has ever seen." The more effusive challenged Branson, Missouri—or even Nashville—to hold a candle to it.

One of the last people to come was Sarah Jo, who shuffled in almost briskly, still without her walker. Her withered cheeks were pink and her faded eyes sparkled. "Oh Mr. Braden, I'm so glad I caught you. I just had to tell you: Mary Ellen Walters just told me she's going to nominate me to be Vice President of our chapter of the Daughters of the Confederacy! And it's all down to you, Mr. Braden. Mary Ellen said she never would have guessed I was such a natural-born leader if she hadn't seen it with her own eyes." Sarah Jo straightened up proudly as she let this sink in.

Fred Hollifield stuck his hoary head round the door. "If you're ready, Braden, we're fixin' to start the second half . . . "

"Oh heavens! Don't let me keep you. I do apologize," and Sarah Jo shuffled hurriedly out to Lydie, who was waiting in the hallway with the walker.

Braden put his red-sequined cummerbund, blue satin bowtie, and tux jacket back on, and then he and Fred walked down the hall toward the sanctuary together. "Well Braden," said the reverend, giving him a fatherly pat on the back, "You've done us proud. More than that, it appears your efforts have found favor in the eyes of the Lord."

"They have?" Braden was mystified.

"Haven't you noticed? The power's on again, and the sun's out, too."

"Thank you Jesus," Braden said, sincerely.

#

The second half was an unqualified success from the moment the orchestra struck up the entr'acte, "When Johnny Comes Marching Home." Cyrus Buell, his eyes wider than ever at the solemnity of the occasion, reverently conveyed our nation's vulnerability as its core Christian values were attacked from forces within as well as without, and the crowd responded with an earnest emphasis on "under God" in the Pledge of Allegiance. This paved the way for a respectful hearing of "The Battle Hymn of the Republic," with the choir newly restored to resonance, and the climactic reappearance of Yolanda, clutching lilies to her ample bosom as she sang of their beauty.

Primed for the offering (accomplished to the strains of "Onward Christian Soldiers" mixed with Mouret's Rondeau), the audience heaped the collection plates. The military tribute was triumphant and sparkling and solemn all at once, and nobody in the orchestra accidentally got a chair on the rolled flag, which unfurled and ascended suddenly to oohs and aahs as the "Star Spangled Banner" arrangement reached its conclusion. Finally, just as the audience were thinking they couldn't possibly have asked for more and looking around in the pews for stray children and belongings, the last chord ended, and two confetti cannons, one on each side of the orchestra, blasted out red, white and blue bits of paper and a few streamers for a crowning delight.

After another hooting, hollering, and stomping ovation, the audience went out into the now sunny afternoon in the elevated state reached in other places at the middle stage of a cocktail party. Voices were raised, faces flushed. Little boys exclaimed over the bang of the cannon at the end—"I was like, 'Ahh!'"—and put their hands over their ears as they staggered around through the leftover puddles in histrionic shock, delighting equally in the memory of the show and their newfound liberty. Little girls made sashes out of the longer bits of crêpe paper the cannons had shot out and pushed their brothers when they fell into them ("Quit actin' like a durn fool, Shane!"). Their daddies had forgotten for a moment their office jobs and expanded figures, and they were unusually solicitous of their wives, who, if not soothing babies startled by the cannon, were looking at their husbands with unusual admiration and gratitude, for although the world was newly perilous and fragile, at least their men were men, and they would stand up for their country against the infidels and their mysterious hatred.

The elderly couples stood straighter and taller, as if their stiff bodies were a palisade against would be invaders. They remembered other threats—the Depression, World War II, Korea, and the '60s, when the whole country had gone wild—and they knew that now as at those other times they would bend, if necessary, only to spring up straighter and taller and prouder than ever before.

The singles had temporarily shed their protective shells and were laughing about how the cannon had startled them or humming their favorite tunes to one another. The men slapped each other on the back, and several boasted mettlesomely of Uncle Sam's military prowess, as though their own virility were at stake. The couples who were progressing in intimacy experienced satisfaction that the cannon had driven them together, causing the women to clutch artlessly at their male escorts and the men to place their arms around the women in equally involuntary protective gestures. Even those who felt things were not working out between them recognized a fellow patriot in their partners and gratefully buried their differences in a shared concern for their country.

As for the old ladies, little and not so, all their cheeks, like Sarah Jo's, were pink, and they looked easily ten years younger as droves of them paused before exiting so as to join the throng around the music minister, renewing the tributes of intermission. "*What* did you do to the choir to get them to sound like that?" "That Yolanda Tibbets is a treasure. I couldn't get *over* it." "I believe our Mr. Braden could even give Branson, Missouri a run for their money. Don't you think so, Ruth?" "Oh I do. I *do*." Several of them pulled Braden to them and planted kisses on him.

Through it all, Brenda and his mother stood back graciously with the other ministers, eyes shining as they absorbed their fair share of reflected glory. Finally the tail end trickled out and Tara Miller graciously allowed Brenda to hurl her plump frame at her fiancé. "I'm so proud of you," she gasped into his ear, enveloping him. Braden squeezed her back and looked over her shoulder, wondering where Jim Engels had got to.

VIII THE PATH TO PATH TO JUDGMENT

If the "Power of Jesus" sermon had opened fire in the Jesus Wars, the Fourth of July Celebration was a devastating counterattack. The entire town was talking about it, there was an upsurge in membership at JUMC, and just when the buzz was threatening to die down, the whole performance was broadcast on local cable, reigniting enthusiasm. For a time Braden was an area celebrity, and *Butler County Living* did a glossy spread on the new impresario, featuring Braden with his choir, Yolanda, various city fathers, and Brenda.

None of this sat well with Hunter Long as he presided over a meeting with Minister of Music King Holloway III, better known as Trip, and Youth Minister Chase Moore at a long table in a conference room of First Baptist's Family Life Center. "I'm not gonna lie to you," Pastor Long began in subdued tones, after they had all gotten coffee. "What really gets my goat about this"—he tapped the latest issue of *Butler County Living* with a well-manicured finger—"what really bothers me—is that nobody is asking the single most important question, my friends, and I think we all know what that is."

"Why didn't *we* think of puttin' on a show?" blurted Trip Holloway, who was something of a wag.

Pastor Long ignored him magnificently. "The single most important question, my friends—and I don't mind telling you, it's one that keeps me up nights—is, 'How many souls were brought to Jesus?' And I think we all know the answer, don't we, friends? I think each one of us knows ex*act*ly how many souls accepted Jesus Christ as their personal savior after *this*." He picked up the magazine by one corner and held it up with distaste so that the image of Braden in front of the choir and Yolanda swung back and forth before the lesser ministers.

Chase Moore's face went pastier than usual behind his owlish spectacles, and he nodded vehemently in agreement with his boss. Despite the appearance of his glasses, he was no raptor, like Pastor Long, but more of a mouse, or perhaps a rat, and his life was divided between scurrying around in accordance with the dictates of his appetites and seeking safety in concealment. Now he felt he must say something, anything, to squirm out from under the keen raptor eyes of Pastor Long, which seemed always on the verge of penetrating to his quivering heart.

"I'm thinkin' maybe you're both right," he said, and immediately regretted it as Pastor Long's gaze only bored deeper, and even Trip Holloway focused on him inquiringly.

Chase's internal sense that he was thrashing around, desperate to break free, manifested itself in a stutter. "It's j-just, maybe we could do a Judgment House? They were t-talkin' about it at that youth ministers' retreat I went t-to—"

"Chase, I think you just might be onto something here," Pastor Long said, now penetrating deep into the youth minister's soft core. "Trip—a" without taking his gaze from Chase, he snapped his long fingers in the direction of the music minister, who had his laptop in front of him. "Search for 'Judgment House.' Find me some detailed descriptions. Chase—talk to me."

As Trip got busy, Chase babbled all he knew: how in each room a scenario was enacted, leading up each time to the question of whether the characters and audience would choose Jesus as their savior; how the audience were forced to watch the characters who had rejected Jesus suffer the consequences of wrong choices, consequences that culminated in the "Hell" room; and how they were finally led to the "Heaven" room, where the saved characters, as well as departed loved ones, were ushered into the everlasting bliss of God's presence. Chase did not stutter as he poured this out, knowing it would save him for now.

When he was finished, and when Trip had corroborated from his laptop findings, Pastor Long sat back in his chair and pressed his fingertips together thoughtfully. "It's a good idea," he said. "But it's too complicated. Because, friends, the most beautiful thing about salvation is how very simple it is. You don't need to think and consider, 'cause in the end the only judgment that matters is God's. And that's what we've got to get people to understand if we're gonna win souls to Jesus Christ. Tell me, have you guys read any of that *Left Behind* series?"

"No, but I've heard somethin' about it," said Trip, who was not much of a reader.

Chase nodded his head and made a mental note to read the books, or at least find out about them, at his earliest opportunity.

"Good man," Pastor Long said, in Chase's direction. "And you—"he pointed an admonitory finger at Trip. "Get to readin'."

"Yes *sir*," said Trip, typing a note into his laptop.

"See, what I like about *Left Behind* is, it shows absolutely how simple our choice as Christians is. Because it's easy for people to get caught up in their everyday problems and forget that one day there will be only one single solitary decision in our whole entire lives that makes one whit of difference, and that is—I don't need to tell *you*, my friends—the decision to accept Jesus Christ as our personal savior.

"Now, the beauty of *Left Behind*, as I see it, is it cuts right to the chase. Timothy Lahaye says, 'Look. What*ever* problems you are dealing with right now, just forget about 'em, because, friends, you got somethin' bigger to worry about, come Judgment Day.'

"And what I'm envisioning here is that we take our cue from Mr. Lahaye, but we go him one better. How? Very simple. We're gonna *show* people what *Left Behind* just talks about. Anymore people won't have to *read* about the biggest decision we are called upon to make in our lives. They will *experience* its consequences firsthand. So let's make sure this is one experience they never forget."

#

And so Path to Judgment was born. It consisted of a forty-five-minute ramble over a winding course of horrific catastrophes, culminating in a Judgment Enclosure. Luraleen and John Whitfield had recently purchased a small farm south of town that was an ideal site for this experience, and volunteers set to work. They converted the barn and immediate vicinity into an orientation area where snacks, souvenirs, porta potties, and ministerial staff would be available, and where Pastor Long would give an introductory address. They cleared paths; they erected stalls to represent a hospital, the Oval Office, etc.; and of course they constructed the Judgment Enclosure, whose design was known only by Pastor Long in its entirety. The workers were sworn to secrecy and told only the bare minimum needed to complete their tasks.

Unlike Braden, Hunter Long and his minions did not need to stoop to wheedling prominent citizens. First Baptist Church was full of exactly the right talent for the occasion. Many men had pickups and experience clearing brush and doing minor construction or electrical work. Sam Braxton, of Sam's Pizza and a cousin to the Braxtons of Braxton Mills, had a small private plane he liked to fly on the weekends that he agreed to lend, especially after Pastor Long explained to him that the popularity of this thing would be such that Sam would be far too busy with the restaurant to go anywhere during the month of October. Winston Hardacre, who went by "Sarge" and owned Good Shoots, the local paintball and laser tag facility, agreed to design and oversee the battlefield, heaven, and hell special effects at a reduced rate, and Macy Munroe, who homeschooled her seven children while her husband (Sarah Jo's nephew) ran the food service over at NWGSU, volunteered to sew and do makeup with her oldest two girls.

At first, Chase Moore was overwhelmed by his duties as casting director, scriptwriter, and drama coach. In the end, though, casting, at least, went relatively smoothly. Chase had been afraid that everyone would want to be an angel or something, but a surprising number volunteered to be devils, infidels, or Horsemen of the Apocalypse (horses courtesy of Shady Ridge Farms Riding Academy, whose proprietor was a deacon), which made Chase think that perhaps he was not the most unclean, creeping hypocrite in the congregation after all. Others happily fell into roles for which they had uniforms and equipment—doctors, nurses, paramedics, police officers, postal workers, veterans, and members of the National Guard. Even in cases where there were more volunteers for a role than were needed on any given night, the number of performances—four times a night every Friday and Saturday night in October, weather permitting—allowed for several actors to take turns in the production.

The script gave Chase the most sleepless nights. Of course much of it could be improv, such as the moans, screams, and cries for help in the initial rapture scene or the agonized pleas by plague victims. Sarge Hardacre's son Mike, who helped out his dad and ran the Taekwondo studio, kindly offered to help choreograph the war scene. Pastor Long also dropped some helpful hints: for instance, he indicated that Timothy Lahaye's idea of making the head of the United Nations be the Anti-Christ seemed like a plausible possibility, and one that would help people understand the dangers inherent in that institution.

But what did a harried, not-righteous-enough-to-be-raptured President of the United States *say* to the Anti-Christ, exactly? It was all right for Timothy Lahaye—he had pages and pages in which to develop characters and situations. On the Path to Judgment, each station could take up no more than ten minutes.

And even more worrisome, because they hit close to home, were the problems of the Judgment Enclosure. Pastor Long decreed that all manifestations of God should be in the form of pure beams of white light from Sarge Hardacre's lasers, but whose disembodied voice should be heard judging? And (Chase shivered just thinking of it) what would He say? And what of the open scoffers, the unbelievers, seduced by the Anti-Christ—what would *they* say? For that matter, what would he, Chase Moore, a believer seething inwardly with foul corruption—what would *he* say when his time came? How could he save himself?

It was late, and Chase was home alone in front of the computer, enveloped in inner and outer darkness, the only light coming from the screen. He pulled his bony knees up under his chin and briefly put his head down on them. Then, as if compelled by Satan, he typed his username into the chat room:

Southern Comfort: Hello everyone!

Lonlygrl: tsup?

The next day an exhausted and extra-guilty Chase was relieved when Jeff Randle, the associate pastor, came back from his vacation and took over the bulk of the script, leaving Chase with only directing duties.

#

Of course, JUMC was aware of all these preparations. The Whitfields and many other families of FBCJ had Methodist friends and acquaintances, and it was hardly possible to drive by the Whitfield farm without noticing the traffic and construction. At this early stage of the Jesus Wars, however, the Methodists believed they had made a sufficient statement with their great show. Besides, they could scarcely credit the outlandish rumors about the Path's substance and purpose. They thought of Path to Judgment, when they thought of it at all, as a Halloween diversion for teenagers. Only later did they come to understand it as part of Pastor Long's visionary drive to dominate the moral and spiritual culture of Jubilee.

All the while, tickets sold like hotcakes, helped along by the united efforts of the entire congregation. Luraleen Whitfield and Sandra Briggs put up posters in His Word, Jubilee Hardware, and around town. John Whitfield, who helped out with fundraising at WGNR, Good News Radio, in return for mentions of His Word, got Path to Judgment put on the station's "Christian Calendar," and had Pastor Long interviewed on a program about Christian alternatives to Halloween.

Publicity was furthered by a number of sinkholes that opened in and around Jubilee in the wake of the tremors, the most momentous of which swallowed a motorcycle belonging to Delia Rosenbaum. Although this was not the biggest or most damaging of the sinkholes, for the purposes of Path to Judgment it ticked all the boxes, since Delia was descended from an established Jewish family in Atlanta but had left even their incomplete faith behind, choosing instead to bring her big-city, militantly lesbian ways to quiet Jubilee, where she became the town's only outspoken atheist. She also spoke out on other matters, and in fact, in her capacity as a geology professor specializing in seismic activity, had been actively engaged in linking the sinkholes to the quarry outside of town at the time of the accident. As the quarry had been Jubilee's most profitable industry since the closure of Braxton Mills' factories, Delia's theories did not sit well with the community, and Pastor Long had only to hint delicately about divine retribution in a sermon for his flock to put two and two together.

IX END TIMES ON PARADE

At last all was ready. Parking areas were designated. The barn roof was repaired, folding chairs were brought in for people to sit in during Pastor Long's introductory speech, tables were set out for displaying refreshments, souvenirs, and other merchandise, and porta potties were rented. Paths had been cleared and stalls built.

Along the first segment of the Path that ticket-holders would experience, representing the initial confusion of the rapture, were damaged cars, an old school bus, and a former ambulance donated by Jubilee Towing and Salvage, whose owner, Russell ("Rusty") Turner, was a longtime FBCJ member. Sam Braxton's plane was also there, positioned at an angle near a wrecked car to suggest a collision. The Jubilee Police Department had lent a recently retired car to help simulate inadequate emergency services.

The next stop, to be introduced by the first Horseman of the Apocalypse, was the Oval Office, where the President was to be slaughtered by the Horseman's arrows after defying the Anti-Christ and proclaiming his faith in Jesus. A bugle call would then direct attention to the second Horseman, high on a hill and backlit by a bonfire. His steed would wear a red sequined caparison that had taken Macy Munroe and her daughters a whole week to complete. With his large sword, this Horseman would point to a spot round a sharp bend in the path; then, spurring his charger, he would unfurl an Islamic banner featuring a gold crescent moon and star against a red backdrop. (Older members of the Four Horsemen committee had wanted to include a hammer and give the moon a sickle handle, but this was deemed too much work for Macy and her daughters.)

Sarge Hardacre was roundly commended for his generosity in lending the tank for the war scene. It was only a 3/5-scale replica of a Sherman tank, but coming suddenly out of the darkness at some distance and emitting appropriately devastating explosive bursts, it was considered plenty convincing. Sarge had built it for fun in his spare time, and he made a little money renting it out for special occasions. For its role in Path to Judgment he refused to accept a penny.

Pastor Long had sat down with Chase to explain his vision for the war scene. First, the audience would be herded into a trench "for their safety" (they'd be told), and they would witness the battle from there, as if they were being held in reserve behind the lines. In front of them, a brave army in camouflage, flying an American flag, would seem to be doing well. Only one would fall under the hail of gunfire from the enemy, who would loudly proclaim their hatred for Jesus. They could also shout Muslim prayers, Pastor Long said, but as he explained, "Allah" was actually just their word for God, so if people shouted "Praise Allah!" they should immediately follow it with "Death to Christians!" or some such clarifying phrase.

Just as the American troops were advancing, however, from the back of the scene Sarge's tank would roll forward with a huge new army. A whine of aircraft would also be heard. The audience would be told to "Get down!" and large explosions would follow.

The tide of battle would turn against the brave Americans. Papier-mâché limbs would fly high in the air ("We're not gonna sugarcoat this thing"). The Islamic troops would redouble their praise of Allah and yell out that he was "coming," while the Americans would cry out warnings against the Anti-Christ.

Knife and hand-to-hand combat would ensue as the remaining Americans made a doomed stand. Exciting action, choreographed by Mike Hardacre, would occur all over the field, culminating in a young hero gruesomely stabbed to death. With his last breath, he would proclaim his love for Jesus, only to be shouted down by his murderer, proclaiming the advent of the Anti-Christ.

"But wait," said Pastor Long, holding up a hand. "All is not lost, my friends." (Chase was the pastor's only auditor, but he could tell from the visionary gleam in his boss' eye that imaginary visitors at the war attraction were being addressed.) "All is not lost because a cry rises out of the darkness—'To the Cross! Go to the Cross! Come to Jesus! We will die for Christ!'"

On a small knoll built for the occasion, a large wooden cross would suddenly be spotlighted. A band of survivors would make their way there, some crawling, many staggering from wounds. Then, placing their backs against it, they would be slaughtered one by one by the forces of the Anti-Christ, each calling out his love for Jesus as he died.

Only then would the audience be told by a dying officer to "get out of the trench and go to the hospital—if you can." On their way, the third Horseman, on his black steed, would join them. Suddenly a mother would emerge, clutching a baby, towing along another child and pushing a cart donated by the Piggly Wiggly that would be filled with Monopoly money. Deaf to her pleas, the Horseman would force her to relinquish not only all the money, but even the cart itself, laughingly telling her she wouldn't need it as he handed her a half loaf of bread for her and her older child to fight over. Then he would shoo the audience on along the path.

Mounting a rise, they would round another bend and find themselves looking down into a hospital—or rather a large, illuminated wooden platform on which a number of sufferers lay on pallets. Some would be wounded soldiers from the battle, others afflicted with sores and boils, a few lying still, apparently dead. Nurses and a doctor would hurry around, lamenting the dearth of medicine and food, clearly unable to handle the number of patients. Only the nurse who prayed and called out to Jesus would have any soothing effect on the sick and injured, and only on those who prayed with her.

Suddenly a loud knocking would be heard on a door in the backdrop at the rear of the platform. Over the objections of the other medical professionals, the praying nurse would answer the knock, disclosing the desperate mother from before, begging for admittance and blaspheming God.

Explaining that she acted in obedience to Christ, the praying nurse would admit her and her children and do what she could, even sharing her last bit of bread with them. Moved by her sacrifice, the mother and several patients and staff would join in singing "Amazing Grace" as the scene ended.

In the last scene before the Judgment Enclosure, the dead from previous scenes who had expired as believers would be arrayed below a large altar and crucifix—an accident victim from the first scene, the President, dead soldiers, the hymn-singing patients, and a doctor from the hospital, all with red crosses on their foreheads. The fourth Horseman, in a black cloak and on a white steed, would point with a skeleton hand at them while Revelations 6:9-11 was read, with the dead crying out to the Lord, "How long before you will judge and avenge our blood on those who dwell on the earth?" and being told to rest a little longer until their number should be complete by an angel who would come in and drape white robes over them as the lights dimmed on all save the Horseman, now pointing his skeleton finger toward the Enclosure.

Pastor Long had ordered the Judgment Enclosure to be constructed around the Whitfields' pool, which, drained for the winter, would make an excellent hell and was furthermore on the way back to the barn. Ushered inside the mysterious black building, ticket holders would first see a film on Armageddon, the last of the end times, and (briefly) Christ's rule on Earth. Loud in volume and rich in CGI, this would emphasize the power of God's wrath as it justly descended on the earth, eventually killing everything in its path.

After the screen had rolled up like a scroll, the audience would find themselves in dim light, staring at a blank black curtain. Pastor Long would appear spotlighted before them to explain their plight. "So, my friends, we meet again, as we all will on that final day. Folks, up to this point, you had a choice. Yes, even in the darkest hour of the Tribulations, if you were alive and breathin' you could still choose to come to Jesus and live forever in glory with Him.

"But I'm here to tell you that the day will come, maybe sooner than we think, when we can no longer choose if we're gonna live in the love and forgiveness of Christ Jesus or just kinda put that decision off from day to day. My friends, as you experience just this small taste of God's justice we offer here, I pray each and every one of you will ask yourselves: 'Where will I be on Judgment Day? Will I be with the born again believers who accepted Jesus into their hearts and were raptured?' Oh my friends, I hope and pray that you will. But failin' that, do you have the strength to face the end times and turn your heart to Christ? Or will you be among the lost—the bitter, the deluded, the followers of the Anti-Christ?

"Let's take a moment to pray. All eyes closed, every head bowed, 'Oh Lord Jesus, who died on the cross for my sins, I freely confess that I am a sinner, and I know that only You can save me from everlastin' torment. Oh please, Jesus, won't You come into my heart? Won't You grant me Your grace so I may turn from my sinful ways before it's too late? Won't You lead me so that I may not be lost, but live in everlastin' glory with the heavenly host and with You, Lord Jesus, in whose name we pray?—Amen.'

"Now folks, I think you all know the path to God's glory is the straight and narrow one. Tonight there is still time for me to invite you to take that path. Oh, my friends, will I see you on the other side, gloryin' with your friends and loved ones where there is no more loss, no more sorrow, no more pain—but only the love of Jesus our savior? I pray that I will, and I want you to know, friends, as you experience just a taste of the judgment that awaits each and every one of us—make no mistake, my friends—I want you to know that everyone involved in the Path to Judgment ministry is prayin' for you to make the right choice, the only choice that matters."

With that Pastor Long would draw aside the black curtain, revealing a walkway just wide enough for three people to walk abreast, and the Whitfields' pool, partially screened by a translucent curtain. The walkway would be dark, at first lit only by the eerie red fog created by covering the pool light with a red gel and putting dry ice around the edges. From the depths would come terrible screams and maniacal laughter, and through the curtain red and black demonic figures would be glimpsed.

A small group of blasphemers would then suddenly come in—soldiers from the war, patients from the hospital—cursing God and calling on the Anti-Christ. They would scorn and deride Pastor Long, even pushing him aside—yes, he would suffer that indignity—but as they crowded toward the walkway, a voice would be heard calling out, "You are not in the book!"

Simulated lightning would shake the enclosure, there would be an explosion, and when the smoke cleared, the blasphemers would have jumped through the curtain to the mattress covering the pool steps, with some proceeding all the way to the trampoline at the bottom of the deep end, and only an agonized face or voice lifted here or there would testify briefly to their existence before they were pushed and shouted down by the demons.

Then the Tribulation Saints in their white robes would enter, bearing a crucifix, gesturing to everyone to rise and singing "Stand Up for Jesus," while the hell noises were temporarily quelled. At the end of the first verse ("Till ev'ry foe is vanquished, and Christ is Lord indeed"), everyone would be standing. The loud voice would be heard again, but this time it would say, "Look! God's dwelling place is now among the people. He will wipe every tear from their eyes. There will be no more death or mourning or crying or pain for they will be His people and God himself will be with them."

After these words from Revelation, the Tribulation Saints would sing "Come Ye Sinners," and a choir stationed behind white laser lights at the far end of the enclosure, beyond the pool and outside the building, would sing with them. The Saints would invite ticket holders to join in the song and urge them onto the path by beckoning, taking their hands, and helping the disabled. By the chorus ("I will arise and go to Jesus"), the enclosure would reverberate with the music.

As they walked along the first part of the path singing, the sounds of hell would rise from the Whitfields' pool, and some of the torments (mostly burning and mocking demons) would be glimpsed through a scrim, but the Tribulation Saints would make sure nobody messed with the scrim or was able to recognize any denizens of the lake of fire. Only after the pool, as they exited the building and approached the white light, should the Saints start pretending to recognize loved ones and break away to run toward them or just "be with Jesus." Then they would join the choir behind the lasers, who would at this point switch to "Joyful, Joyful We Adore Thee."

Before the audience members could join them, however, an imposing angel would come forward. "Your time is not yet come," he would proclaim, and they would be shunted off to the barn, where they could buy Path to Judgment t-shirts and meet with church members who would guide them on their spiritual journey.

X T. J. ON THE PATH

T. J. Dillingham was nine years old and lived in the Jubilee Meadows subdivision with his mom and dad and his sister, Hannah Grace, who was thirteen. His daddy, Jake, was a police officer. His mamma, Rachel, taught kindergarten at the Sydney Lanier Early Learning Center. She was Chase Moore's half sister.

Jake had put a lot of time into helping clear the trails and build the structures for Path to Judgment, and he was looking forward to taking the kids to admire his handiwork while undergoing a salutary spiritual experience. Rachel wasn't so sure. "You don't think T. J.'s too young?" she asked, pursing her lips so that her pinched features appeared even sharper than usual and looking doubtfully from the Path to Judgment flyer in her hand to her son, who shared his mother's thinness. "It says here, it's not recommended for kids under ten, and that staff will 'remove any young children who seem to be in distress (crying, etc.).'"

"Cryin'!" exclaimed Jake. "My son's not gonna cry—are you, boy?" He slapped him playfully on the back of the head.

"No sir," T. J. said with determination, straightening a little. He was getting good at not crying, he thought, remembering the deer he had shot last fall, how it looked at him, and he thought of his dad and pulled the trigger.

"I know it's tough, Rache, but it's the real truth about what's coming. And the kids need to see it before they get to that age where they think they know better'n us what's good for 'em."

"Oh I agree one hundred percent about *that*. But—" Rachel sat down on a chair and looked into T. J.'s face. "You're not gonna be upset, now, when you see Mommy all bloody comin' outa that bus? You know it's just pretend?" Rachel had signed up to be an accident victim on most nights.

"It's not just pretend, Rachel. Don't tell him that. This here's the real deal, son."

"Yes, but you know your mamma's saved, so I'll be pretending to be another lady who couldn't be raptured 'cause she wasn't saved. You understand?"

T. J. nodded. "Yes ma'am."

His mother looked doubtfully from him to his father. Then she got up. "All right, Jake. If you think he's ready."

"Course he is, aren't ya, boy?"

"Yes sir."

"And no cryin', hear?"

"No sir."

#

The kids sat on hay bales up front for Pastor Long's introductory speech. Hannah Grace sat off with her friends, looking very grown up. There were lots of people T. J. knew from church, but also lots he knew went to other churches, and some he'd never seen before, so he knew the thing was a success, and he was fleetingly proud of his parents for being a part of it.

T. J. didn't attend too well to the pastor's speech. Pastor Long warned that the Path would be scary, and T. J. hoped it would be, but not *too* scary. At least it wouldn't be boring. At this point Whit Randle, always a troublemaker and two years older than T. J., poked him and whispered, "Bet you pee your pants, Dill-Pickle-Ham," and T. J. poked back furtively and whispered, "Bet *you* will, and poop in 'em, too," and moved down off the hay bale onto the floor so Whit couldn't get him in trouble, and when he again picked up the thread of the minister's discourse, Pastor Long was explaining about how all the bad things people would go through in the end times were God's justice that they brought on themselves, and T. J. thought God was kind of like a policeman, like his own dad, only unimaginably bigger and fiercer, and then he thought of how hunting was right, too, because it put meat on the table as God intended, and he couldn't deny that those beautiful deer, with their big eyes and delicate feet, were delicious to sink your teeth into, especially if you had shot them yourself and your dad was proud of you.

Then Pastor Long spoke about the path to salvation and how each and every one had to actively choose to "embrace Jesus in your heart and let His love into your life," and T. J. saw that Hannah Grace had stopped whispering with her friends and was sitting up very straight and proud because she had been baptized last year, and when Pastor Long was praying T. J. thought of all the sin he had in him, especially not honoring his parents all the time, and wondered if he would be truly saved when the time came or would just man up and go through with it, like with the deer, even though God would know.

After the prayer they trooped out in a group of about thirty. It was dark, but the scene was lit up by the lights of vehicles either stranded when their drivers were raptured or stuck in an accident or traffic jam. Car horns and sirens were going, injured people were staggering around or just stuck in vehicles, and family members sought one another in vain. Suddenly T. J. saw his mother coming toward him, only of course he knew it wouldn't be her when the time came because she would be raptured.

"Somebody help!" she screamed, fake blood streaming down her face. "Oh please, why can't somebody *help* us?"

"Sorry, Mrs. D.—too late now," Whit called out from behind T. J., and Mr. Dillingham turned around, but Mrs. Randle was on it.

"Whitford Beauregard Randle—*what* did we talk about before we came?"

"Sorry. Won't happen again," Whit rejoined blithely.

"Won't happen again *what*?"

"Won't happen again, ma'am."

"I swear, sometimes I think this child is just *askin'* for a whuppin'," Mrs. Randle said plaintively to the group.

"Oh well. You know what they say about preachers' kids," said T. J.'s daddy, and he ruffled T. J.'s hair proudly.

Soon his mother was elbowed aside by other injured parties. T. J. dawdled enough to see her stagger towards the empty ambulance stuck in the traffic jam but collapse before she got there. Drivers honked their horns and told her to "git outa the road, lady!"

As they got to the quieter place on the path, just before the Oval Office, T. J. took a few hurried steps and caught up with Hannah Grace, who was walking with just Jenna Whitfield because their other friends were in the next group. "Hey, Hannah Grace, wait up," he said.

She turned with an exasperated look, like he'd been pestering her all day long, but he still had to ask, "It's just—there was all those people. How come nobody helped Mamma?" Too late he felt his father come up behind him. As Hanna Grace rolled her eyes and explained to Jenna that he was "just a kid," his dad gave him another playful slap on the back of the head.

"Weren't you listening to Pastor Long, boy? All the true Christians been raptured up to be with the Lord. Ain't enough good people left *to* help. But like we told you, you ain't got to worry. In real life your mamma's saved. You got that?"

T. J. nodded, though he felt somehow that his question hadn't really been answered. "Yes sir."

XI T. J. IN THE END TIMES

The Oval Office did not make much of an impression. T. J. enjoyed seeing Clayton Briggs, already portly and now heavily padded, fall under a hail of arrows from the Horseman of the Apocalypse, but he did not even try to follow all the palaver beforehand about the Jews and their temple and the Anti-Christ.

He liked the red horse, and at first the war scene was thrilling. The Muslims seemed to be coming right at their group in the trench, yelling, "Death to Christians! Allah be praised!" and "Death to the infidels!"

Just in front of them were the Americans, the Whitfields' son Chuck, in his National Guard uniform, urging them on with "God bless America!" and "Fight for Christ!" while occasionally telling the audience to "Get down!" Everybody was cheering, and when the tank came up over the ridge T. J. thought at first it was going to finish off the unbelievers.

This was clearly not the case, as Chuck keeled over, bleeding profusely, in the first round of explosive fire. Whit, who had been quiet for a while (only, T. J. thought, because it was hard to compete with the noise of the battle), said loudly, "Aww, he can't die. Yo, Cap'n Chuck! Wake up!" but there was no response, and Whit was soon distracted by more explosions.

The only other commentary came from Hannah Grace, who said, "Eww, gross," when a papier-mâché limb fell too close to the trench.

Then one especially brave American threw a grenade that stopped the tank, and they all cheered again, but as the enemy closed in it became painfully apparent that the remnant of Americans were outnumbered. Hannah Grace put her hands over her eyes and peeked at the slaughter through her fingers, and Whit said, "Aw—that's so fake" whenever an American fell, but T. J. just stood up straighter and watched like he knew his father wanted him to.

Suddenly a young man was stabbed just in front of them. T. J. saw that it was Zach Finley, who sang praise songs on some Sundays with his band.

Zach's attacker said, "Where's yer Jesus now?" as he drove the knife in, and blood spurted out, even getting a few drops on the audience.

Zach did not reply, but gestured toward the hill on which the cross was now illuminated and fell to his knees, calling on Jesus before expiring.

By the time the martyrs were falling around the cross, Jenna was trying to get Hannah Grace to stop crying so they wouldn't be thrown out, and T. J.'s father patted him on the back and bent down to say in his ear, "Don't worry, son. They're all going to be with Jesus," but T. J. just felt kind of numb. There was still too much noise (mainly cheers for Allah and the Anti-Christ) to really think about stuff anyway.

It felt good to get back on the path again, and though T. J. was a little spooked by the third Horseman, he knew the story of the high-priced bread from Sunday school and so was prepared when the poor woman had her buggy taken away with all the money in it. Still, it was shocking to see her and the little kid (whom he didn't know) fighting over the bread. T. J. was far from perfect, but he felt that if push came to shove he'd starve and let his mamma have every last crumb, especially if she was nursing a baby brother or sister. But then again, he thought, his mamma would certainly insist that he have some and not let him give it to her. She was a regular bear about a balanced breakfast. As far as his daddy was concerned—well, T. J. simply wouldn't dare fight *him*.

As they walked on, T. J.'s mind wandered, and he thought that since just about all the Baptists would be raptured up, the woman who fought over the bread with her kid would have to be Methodist or Presbyterian or Episcopal or some kind of wacko like Delia What's-her-face. He tried to imagine the people he knew, like Miss Walters, his teacher, behaving like that. It just didn't seem likely, he thought, shaking his head as he trudged uphill. But then, starvation could probably do some strange things to people.

When they came up to the top of the rise and looked down into the hospital, T. J. was shocked to see his mother, her face pale with a smear of blood, lying among the dead. He supposed they had told him, but he had forgotten until now.

Whit bumped into him accidentally on purpose. "Looks like your mom didn't make it," he said, shaking his head in mock sadness.

After that T. J. was distracted by all the things he would have done to Whit if his father weren't right there and if Whit weren't so much bigger than T. J. was, and so he didn't pay much attention, though he got the gist of the scene. It was a relief to go away and not look at his mom anymore, though she did a good job and you could hardly see her breathing.

There was a bit of a walk from the hospital to the altar scene, and Whit, who was plump and out of shape, fell behind. T. J. pretended to have a stone in his shoe and stopped, his heart pounding. This would never work, he thought, but when Whit came jogging past, trying to catch up, T. J. stuck his foot out, and Whit fell beautifully face forward into the dust and gravel.

Somehow, though, it did not feel as satisfying as T. J. had thought it would, especially as Whit immediately scrambled up yelling, "Hey! He tripped me!"

"It was an accident, I swear," T. J. lied desperately, as they came up to the grown-ups. "I was just standing up after I got that stone outa my shoe, and I just didn't see him." He refrained from adding another "I swear," which would have overdone the thing, but on an inspiration, he turned and proffered his hand to Whit. "Sorry, man."

Seeing his mother's sharp eyes on him, Whit took the hand, but squeezed it hard and gave T. J. a look that told him this was by no means over.

"That's right, boys, make it up," T. J.'s father said, but later, in an aside to T. J., he muttered, "Probly had it coming," and patted T. J. on the shoulder.

The fourth Horseman was the most awesome. He was so closely shrouded in his cloak that T. J. could not tell who he was, and the skeleton hand glowed in the dark as it pointed at the martyrs. T. J.'s mother was not among them, but Whit made no comment on this. T. J. assumed he was busy plotting his revenge.

The angel was clearly Mrs. Melanie Long, the pastor's wife. T. J. always felt bad when he saw her because he didn't like her, though he didn't know why. If anyone had ever asked him, all he could have come up with was that she was too sweet, and that was no reason. But like now, for instance. Why did she have to smile all the time? Would the angel handing out white robes to the Tribulation Saints really be wearing the same smile Mrs. Long used when handing out paint smocks in vacation bible school?

The glowing skeleton hand pointed to the mysterious Judgment Enclosure. T. J. was very excited to see this, since everyone had been talking about how awesome it was. T. J.'s daddy had helped put it up, but when T. J. asked he said he honestly didn't know much about it, but even if he did, he wasn't allowed to talk about it.

It was a little disappointing to have just a movie at first, but it was a long building, so T. J. knew there'd be more to come. He picked a seat surrounded by people. Hannah Grace was clearly annoyed that he was sitting so close to her and her friend, but T. J. reasoned correctly that by the time Mrs. Randle finished warning Whit to "behave himself in there" and came in, they would have to sit somewhere in the back, out of range.

The movie was pretty scary. It talked about God's wrath in the Flood times and showed how God's wrath was going to come again and tip over all the skyscrapers in earthquakes and flood things and afflict people with sores and burns. It said He'd kill everything in the sea, and finally just incinerate the whole world.

T. J.'s Nanna and Pop Pop had an old family bible with a picture of the Flood where people were desperately trying to save themselves on a medium-sized rock. Swimming up alongside of the rock was a tigress. With the same desperation as the woman with the baby on the other side, the tigress was trying to deposit her cub on the rock, but you could tell that in another moment the waves were going to wash them all down into the depths.

T. J. had always been fascinated by that picture when he was little, especially after his Nanna explained to him about the Flood. He felt sorry for the tiger family, and even a little sorry for the human one, though the bible clearly said they were too wicked to live. But how could a tigress be wicked? He wondered how the pairs of animals were chosen for the ark, and why the tigress hadn't made the cut, and whether he would draw God's wrath down on himself just for wondering.

Now T. J. wondered about the sea creatures. What had the whales done to deserve God's wrath? He must just trust that God had a plan for them, but still it bothered him. It was like when his father told him to do something and he asked why and his father said, "Because I said so. That's why."

Then the movie was over and Pastor Long came out and prayed with everybody, and T. J. prayed that God would accept his own rebellious and sinful heart and save him one day, just as He had Hannah Grace.

XII T. J. AND THE LAST JUDGMENT

The lights and sound came on, and they could see hell through the curtain. It was fascinating. If he hadn't known it was the Whitfields' swimming pool, T. J. thought, he would never have guessed. It just looked like this big hole with a red mist coming out of it and a couple of red and black figures lying around it, but the noises that came out of the depths were tough to listen to.

The unbelievers came in, jeering at Christians in general and Pastor Long in particular. They looked terrible—all wounded and burned and covered with sores and blood and blackened skin—and they blamed it all on God. But what they didn't notice was that behind the curtain the dark figures had gotten up and started to dance around, and demonic laughter filled the speakers.

Then the God haters went too far. When they pushed Pastor Long, who was just practically begging them to repent while there was still time, suddenly there was a lightning flash through the air, and thunder rolled. A voice called out, "You are not in the book!" and a puff of smoke ("Awesome," said Whit, before being consumed with fake coughing), and the mockers disappeared through the curtain panels, whereupon new screams arose from the hell pool. When people tried to get out, T. J. could hear the demons laughing and see them pushing the sinners back down with pitchforks. He couldn't really see what was happening to the mockers, though, which was disappointing but probably for the best, he thought.

Then the light of the hell pool seemed to dim, and a bunch of Tribulation Saints came in, carrying a big cross and singing "Stand up for Jesus." They handed out photocopies from the hymnal and gestured to everybody to stand up with them and join in, and everybody did. T. J. could hear old Mrs. Farrow's soprano quavering out over everyone. His family had all had a chuckle when T. J.'s daddy had told his mamma about how Mrs. Farrow's son Clint tried to stop her going because FBCJ was allowing "coloreds" and whites on the Path together, but old Mrs. Farrow just told him to mind his own business. Mrs. Farrow was eighty-seven and dead set on coming, even though all the Farrows were Primitive Baptists. She refused to use a walker, but leaned on the arm of her handsome great-grandson, Dusty Mathers, especially going up the hills.

The loud voice announced about God dwelling with the people and no one ever dying or being sad again, and Dusty and Mrs. Farrow sang out "Amen" afterwards, Mrs. Farrow louder. Then some people in the front started saying, "Look!" and pointing down the long, narrow passage, and T. J. dodged in between the bigger people and saw beyond the Saints, who were blocking the passage, a white light coming from the end of it, just as everyone heard a choir start up with "Come Ye Sinners."

The Saints began herding everyone into the passageway, and they were all singing "I will arise and go to Jesus" and trying to see what was going on in the hell pool. T. J. saw a demon with a long whip on the edge of the pool, and a hideously burned face coming up out of it, and he heard a woman screaming and thought he saw her being stabbed over and over again.

Too late he heard, "Go to hell, Dildoham," in his ear, and Whit pushed him hard into the scrim. There was a small space between the walkway and the metal bar weighting the bottom of the scrim, and as his shoulder collided with it and it gave but did not break, T. J. felt his sneaker catch in the space, and then something grabbed his foot.

For a split second he panicked and thought he might be willing to leave his shoe behind and take a whipping just to get free, but as he looked down into the space, he felt the hand pushing up on his shoe, and he saw the same hideously blackened face that had popped up at him a minute ago. "Not yet!" the face moaned at him, and with an agonized howl it let go and sank back into the misty red depths.

The singing stopped as T. J. righted himself. "You OK, son?" asked one of the Saints, Mr. Jenkins, who was a friend of T. J.'s dad.

"Yes sir," said T. J. He was satisfied to see another Saint hustling Whit along to the exit up ahead, but at the same time he thought he would never be all right again till he was saved.

"Thatta boy," said Mr. Jenkins, and patted T. J. on the shoulder. Abruptly up ahead, one of the Saints called out, "Mamma—is that you? Wait for me—I'm coming!" and she ran down a little ramp, through an open set of double doors and across a stretch of lawn toward the white laser light that had lit up the passage. T. J. thought he could see figures behind it.

Quickly the other Saints began calling out and running too. "Jesus—I'm comin' home!" Mr. Jenkins hollered, as he let go of T. J.'s shoulder and took off.

T. J. was left with just the audience members. They had all followed the Saints down the ramp and were standing outside the doors looking toward the light. T. J. looked up at old Mrs. Farrow, who was standing beside him, tears streaming down her wrinkled cheeks. On her other side, T. J. saw Dusty take her old veiny hand and stroke it gently. "You don't got too long to wait now, do you Nan Nan?" he said, in a low voice. She shook her head and just let the tears fall.

Behind the light the choir broke into "Joyful, Joyful," just as an angel came forward, looking stern. "Your time is not yet come," he announced, and shunted them all off onto a path leading back to the barn.

When they got there, T. J. was relieved to see that Whit's mother must have hauled him off home already. Hannah Grace immediately spotted her friends who had tickets for the next time slot, and she and Jenna went over to tell them how awesome it was. T. J. just felt kind of dazed after the whole thing and didn't want to talk much. His daddy, who was in a good mood, approved. "You got a lot to think about, doncha, boy?" he said, ruffling T. J.'s hair again.

"Yes sir," T. J. agreed, nodding. His daddy bought Path to Judgment t-shirts for the whole family and a camo Path to Judgment hunting cap for T. J. Hannah Grace bought 4Him's latest CD with her own pocket money.

T. J. didn't have enough money to buy anything, but the stuff they were selling wasn't that interesting anyway. He wished he had his Gameboy from the truck, but he knew he was supposed to be thinking deep thoughts, so he didn't ask if he could go get it but just mooned around pretending to look at the pamphlets his Uncle Chase was handing out to the youth and then at the *Veggie Tales* DVDs and such. He tried not to think about the soldier's blood spurting out, or his mamma lying dead, or the woman being stabbed everlastingly in the hell pool, or how he felt when his foot was grabbed. He wondered why hell and all the bad things were so much more interesting than the heaven part, but he supposed it was because he was sinful. When his father thought the kids weren't looking, T. J. saw him buy a purity ring for Hannah Grace.

XIII GROWING TENSIONS

Path to Judgment received mixed reviews. On the one hand, 583 souls gave themselves over to Jesus during its run, and hundreds more were reinforced in their belief or assailed in their unbelief—all this despite the show being rained out twice. Visitors had come from throughout the Southeast, a few from even farther away, and the Path had received media coverage from all local news outlets. Takings in ticket sales and revenues from concessions were profitable. All in all, Pastor Long considered Path to Judgment an unqualified success and hoped to see it catch on among his colleagues at ministerial conferences and retreats.

On the other hand, the professional classes of other denominations, including the Methodists, had come to regard Path to Judgment with distaste and even some alarm. Several parents wrote letters to *The Jubilee Sentinel* saying that their teenagers were upset by it, or that they had seen younger children upset, or that it gave a distorted picture of a vengeful God—though supporters also wrote to thank FBCJ for scaring their troubled children straight or just "telling it like it is" about Christianity.

Jim Engels was one of the concerned parents, though he did not write in, as he believed in keeping private concerns private. Lynette had gone through with her boyfriend out of curiosity and declared she wouldn't go back because she believed religion should be about love, but Katie, who was only just thirteen, had come back troubled and silent. Lynette told her parents she thought this was because the guy who had been killed right in front of the trench was that guy, Zach, who had done all that landscaping on the Engels' yard last summer. And they all recalled how Katie had spent a lot of time up in the big magnolia with a book and a pair of binoculars while Zach labored (Jim had been pleased at her sudden obsession with reading), and how she had volunteered to make lemonade and take it out to Zach.

Whatever the cause, Katie changed. She dropped her old friends from the

JUMC youth group and refused to go to choir practice. Instead she took up with the FBCJ girls in the junior high, especially Jenna Whitfield. She quit the school paper and even spent less time on the computer. Instead she holed up in her room reading the bible and other religious literature, listening to contemporary Christian music, and contemplating a large poster of the Newsboys she put up above her bed. She also started attending FBCJ youth group and bible study with Jenna.

Her parents did not like to interfere. They had already been through a similar alienation from Lynette, who still tended to regard them as a sort of annoying talking furniture on the set of her busy life. Judy Engels was even happy to see Katie less absorbed by the computer screen. Jim, who believed the Southern Baptist religion thrived on promoting hatred, took a darker view. He did not speak about this, however, but only prayed that the phase would pass before his daughter learned to abominate all that he was.

#

The ministerial staff at JUMC took no explicit notice of Path to Judgment, thereby ostensibly placing themselves above the Jesus fray. This moral high ground proved an ideal point from which to launch a counter-offensive, however, as it freed them to engage with the international developments that increasingly preoccupied the public mind toward the end of 2002.

It was becoming obvious to all but Delia Rosenbaum and her kind that not only Afghanistan, but Iraq, and beyond it Syria, Lebanon, Yemen, and probably the entire Muslim world, would need to be dealt with. Such, at least, was general understanding of the message delivered at the September 11th Interfaith Memorial Ceremony (held on the Jubilee Town Square) by Cliff Bowman, Assistant to the Deputy Secretary of Homeland Security. Moreover, people were still undergoing extra scrutiny from security at their workplaces, at large events such as football games or concerts, and when traveling.

Altogether, vigilance and proactive defense were in the air, the zeitgeist to which, Braden felt, JUMC's Christmas concert must respond. The problem, as Braden expressed it to Brenda in mid-September on one of her many visits, was that there were not enough good patriotic war songs and hymns with a Christmas angle, or, for that matter, Christmas songs with a militant feel.

They were "cuddling together," as Brenda put it, on a large brown sectional Brenda had bought "for the house," as she alluded to the dwelling they would inhabit after marriage, and so that she could have a "comfy spot" on her visits. This was not, it should be noted, a spot to sleep, as long ago, on her first visit without his mother, in fact, Brenda's patient resistance to Braden's tepid advances had melted away. Now she was leaning her soft, sloppy figure up against him and resting her head on his shoulder, an outward embodiment of the inward oppression Braden felt.

With an effort, he extricated his left arm from under her flesh and put it around her, patting her tenderly. The irony was, he really liked Brenda very much—she was dear to him, his oldest friend, and if only he hadn't been so recently disappointed on other fronts he might even have been able to muster some enthusiasm for their impending romantic interlude. Sex was sex, after all, and he knew he was good at it because she told him so. Maybe it was being detached, he thought. Or maybe it was just because she was so appreciative. He often thought that being a fat girl must be something like being a gay man, socially—you were welcome everywhere, but openly desired?—hardly anywhere.

Now she sighed contentedly and exhibited a rare flash of brilliance. "You're right, honey. Even the songs that *are* military are all about wantin' to be home—like 'I'll be *Home* for Christmas.' Why don't you do a show about what we're defending? You know, home, family, the American way of life."

Braden would have sprung to his feet had he not been weighed down. "Brenda, you're a genius," he said, kissing the top of her head. "'Chestnuts roasting,' 'No Place Like Home,' 'Santa Claus is Coming to Town' for the youth choir. . . ."

She had turned and was looking at him in that encouraging, admiring way she had, beaming with pleasure at his compliment. "And the icing on the cake," he continued, "is that whatever it is they're fixin' to put on over at FBCJ, I'm guessing it's *not* family friendly."

Braden had a vision again. It was so sweet it almost obliterated the cause of his underlying gloom, namely the memory of Alessandro Trentini in the parking lot outside the NWGSU athletic facility, leaning against his Fiat and avoiding eye contact while he finished his cigarette. "Of course, I have enjoyed our times together," he had said, with a gentle smile, "But I have to meet someone tonight." He turned his head, exhaling a fragrant cloud of smoke.

Braden could not read his expression in profile. "Someone special?" he asked, trying not to bleat. They both knew he was clutching at straws.

"Yes," Alessandro said, and stubbed out his cigarette.

The flat finality of it had hung in the air between them as the violinist got out his keys and unlocked the car door with a beep. Braden held up a hand. "Of course, totally understand. I'm the one who should be sorry," he said hurriedly, though Alessandro certainly hadn't apologized. "Like they say, all's fair in love and war." He forced a smile and, after a quick look round the almost empty lot, leaned in for a peck on the cheek and a last whiff of Alessandro's scent of cigarettes and Dior cologne. "*Ciao bello.*"

Mustering his dignity, Braden sauntered to his Dodge Intrepid without a backward glance and settled in unhurriedly, giving Alessandro time to roar out with his customary ridiculous acceleration. Braden knew he would find someone else before too long, but coming as it did on top of Jim's abrupt toning down of anything resembling flirtation, Alessandro's firm refusal to renew their playful encounters was unnerving.

XIV HOME FOR THE HOLIDAYS

In accord with Brenda's suggestion, Braden's Christmas program was a celebration of Christmas at home in four parts. As usual, the bell choir performed the prelude. Still under May Ewing's direction, since Sarah Jo found her new duties with the Daughters of the Confederacy consumed her energies, they played "The Holly and the Ivy," "O Christmas Tree," and "O Come, All Ye Faithful" with military precision. The orchestra also performed a medley of carols for the overture. On the strength of Braden's Fourth of July concerts, sponsors had risen to the occasion—Henderson's BBQ chief among them—and to show there were no hard feelings, Braden used the extra money to contract with Alessandro Trentini for a real string section that provided a lush, nostalgic sound.

After Reverend Hollifield's welcome and opening prayer, the first part of the program began in earnest. It consisted of traditional Gospel readings, illustrated by carols and hymns evoking the Middle East in its comfortable aspect as cradle of Christianity: "Lo, How a Rose E'er Blooming," "O Come O Come Emmanuel," "The First Noel," "O Little Town of Bethlehem," "Joy to the World," and "We Three Kings of Orient Are"—all the old favorites. With the enhanced orchestra they could do beautiful John Rutter arrangements and melt the old ladies' hearts.

Only in the finale of the first half was a quasi-military note introduced. The drum corps of NWGSU, in full regalia, entered the sanctuary from the rear, marching to a military rat-a-tat-tat. Impassively receiving the cheers of the multitude, they paraded up the aisle and across the stage before lining up in formation behind the percussion section of the orchestra and rocking out "Little Drummer Boy" with the choir. The half ended to spirited applause and a few shouts of "Go Bears!"

After intermission the audience was bombarded with evocations of domestic holiday bliss. First the orchestra played "Sleigh Ride." This segued into the version with the words, with soloists Lynette Engels and her friend Mark Thompson, a budding gay tenor whom Braden had taken under his wing. The young couple sat on a wheeled pallet decked out as a sleigh and drawn across the stage by nine children from Rita Hill's Superstarz! Academy, all sporting reindeer antlers (Rudolph, in the front, also had a red nose).

Then there was a full-on celebration of home, with "Deck the Halls" (an audience sing-along), and Walkin' in a Winter Wonderland," "Let it Snow," and "No Place Like Home for the Holidays" appropriately dramatized. Finally, for the offering, the ever-gracious Yolanda Tibbets gave an almost alarmingly sultry rendition of "The Christmas Song" ("Chestnuts roasting by an open fire"? Jim quipped confidentially to Braden later. "I'm not even gonna touch that one with a ten-foot pole. Let's just say I saw a lot of grown men with their faces all aglow.") Collection baskets were heaped with bounty.

Once again, it seemed best to follow Yolanda with children. The youth choir gave a relatively spirited rendition of "Santa Claus Is Coming to Town," with Christopher Hill, Rita's youngest (aged nine), singing about the tin drums and root-a-toot-toots and bringing a little drum and a noisemaker onto the stage.

After loud applause and murmurings over Christopher's cuteness, Braden introduced the military highlight of the program by explaining that great performances like the one they were enjoying could only be put together with a lot of behind-the-scenes work and, above all, discipline. He said that no doubt the audience knew Reverend Hollifield from Sunday services as a loving, concerned pastor, but that there was another, sterner side to him, and he, Braden, would now show how things were *really* run at JUMC, to the tune of Elton John's "Step into Christmas." The audience, Braden reminded them, had the words to the chorus in their programs, and Braden had it on good authority that those who failed to join in would be forced to do push-ups after the concert.

Jim Engels had declined to sport Elton's platform footwear ("Dammit, Braden, I'm not prepared to don any apparel *that* gay!"), but he had consented to have bell bottoms attached to his tuxedo trousers, and over a pair of cowboy boots encrusted with hot-glued rhinestones they had the desired effect as he made his way down from the organ to the piano on one side of the stage. To titters and applause from the audience, he put on a pair of outsized glasses like those Elton John wore, with sprigs of holly adorning each side, and he was then joined by Ron Wylie, who picked up a shiny black electric bass bedecked with silver tinsel. Both men bowed to loud applause and a "You rock, Ronny!" from one of his buddies in the pews.

Before the audience had time to simmer down, Reverend Hollifield entered in a drill sergeant's uniform, his military cap decorated with holly. Marching to the beat of a snare drum, he crossed the stage and picked up the toy drum and noisemaker Christopher Hill had left there, hanging the drum round his neck by its strap and sticking the noisemaker in his mouth.

His hands now free, he struck a "one two, one two" marching beat with the toy drum sticks. Immediately the rest of the ministerial staff marched up on stage in a line, except Marian Hollifield, who was overseeing the youth backstage. All wore soldiers' camo with tinsel adorning their caps, and Reverend Hollifield's niece, Leigh Ann Hollifield, who helped out with the Sunday school, brought up the rear in a red tinsel boa over her uniform.

Reverend Hollifield blew on his noisemaker to bring the troops to attention, and there was laughter as its long red and green tongue uncurled and sprang back again. Braden was still on his podium, but he hurriedly grabbed his own decorated soldier's cap from Brenda, jammed it on his head, and stood stiffly at attention.

Reverend Hollifield faced front and gave another blast on his noisemaker, whereupon his troops likewise turned to the audience. Leigh Ann gave a couple of shimmies with her boa, but straightened up abruptly when she was reprimanded with a stern look and another blast. Looking straight at Braden, Reverend Hollifield delivered an extra-long toot, and Braden signed to Ron to begin the guitar riff before the audience's laughter had a chance to die down.

Reverend Hollifield's high, nasal tenor was appropriate to the singsong delivery of his preaching—which commonly mounted to emphatic peaks of tension before plunging into valleys of resignation—but it was penetratingly unpleasant as a singing voice. Cyrus Buell had no sense of pitch at all and only mumbled out the hymns in an off-key, reticent *Sprechstimme.* Fortunately the opening lines of the song lent themselves to a spoken delivery. With the cheers occasioned by Ron's sexy handling of his guitar still ringing out, Fred Hollifield intoned the introduction, more or less in the confines of the beat, but with his characteristic pausings and tonal vicissitudes bearing no relation to the melody, and then Cyrus rumbled out some lines about a Christmas card in an embarrassed but resonant monotone.

Craig Wright, the youth minister, relieved the situation with his lovely baritone setting up Leigh Ann's tuneful soprano well, and when she shimmied with her boa, inviting the audience to "step into Christmas" with her, a wolf whistle, several "Woo*hoo*!"'s, and a "You go girl!" were heard from the audience.

After Leigh Ann's invitation a pause was inserted, during which the reverend blew a stern blast to restore order, and then Braden turned around to bring in the audience. Everyone sang until the sanctuary rang with "the admission's free-ee-ee!"

Marching forward (in time to the music, Braden noted, with relief), Reverend Hollifield came down the middle of the steps up to the stage, and the others fell into line behind him, Leigh Ann bringing up the rear. As the choir took over the second verse, the reverend's troop marched ahead through the orchestra, and then, each placing their hands on the waist of the minister in front of him (or in Leigh Ann's case, her), they formed a conga line. Putting his baton down, Braden turned to the audience and began clapping his hands together over his head, and soon everyone was clapping with him.

As they passed up the central aisle, the ministers invited people to join them, and after Buddy Wilson, the NWGSU football coach, jumped up and grabbed ahold of Leigh Ann, the pews were rapidly depleted. (Buddy was a popular figure, having just come off a ten and three season.) While those who remained, through shyness or infirmity, kept up the enthusiasm by clapping and singing on the choruses, the conga line snaked around the back of the pews and passed down the side aisle to the door nearest the piano.

Meanwhile on the opposite aisle some envious audience members formed their own conga line, but they had only just gotten to the back of the pews when Braden signaled for the chorus to fade out. Amid cheers and applause, the audience members returned to their seats, happy and out of breath, and Fred Hollifield tooted his troops up on stage and into a quick bow before marching them off and out the side doors.

As the lights dimmed and the audience's excited murmurings died down, Braden gave his military cap back to Brenda and took up the microphone to introduce the fourth and final section of the concert. "That was fun, wasn't it?" he began, briefly reviving the laughter with a little shimmy of his own.

"But we mustn't forget that we're celebrating because of a very *special* joy, and that is, the birthday of our savior, Jesus Christ, the reason for the season. As we sing these next three numbers, the beautiful spiritual, "Mary Had a Baby," the hymn, "What Child Is This," which you may also know as 'Greensleeves,' and finally 'Silent Night,' in an arrangement with Franz Schubert's 'Ave Maria,' we hope that you will remember all the very special blessings we experience at this holy season—the blessing of living in this great country, the blessings of our homes and families and loved ones—but most of all the blessing of our Lord Jesus Christ, who shares all our sorrows and is the source of all our joys. On behalf of all of us here at Jubilee United Methodist, I want to thank you all for sharing this very special season with us.

"We'll conclude with the rousing 'Hallelujah Chorus' from Handel's *Messiah.* We wish you a Christmas filled with the joy of the season and the very happiest New Year. In the words of Charles Dickens' Tiny Tim, 'God bless us, every one!'"

XV LITTLE JOHNNY AND THE WALL OF JERICHO

Though Braden felt JUMC's holiday concert was lacking in excitement, especially when contrasted with its celebration of Independence Day, the event was greeted with unanimous, if mild, enthusiasm. As Braden and Brenda had intended, the audience understood that this holiday season it was their patriotic responsibility to celebrate the many blessings of their homes while not forgetting either the God Who granted them or the troops who kept them secure. Among those blessings they counted the JUMC Christmas concert, which enabled them to fulfill all these obligations in one fell swoop.

But this success rolled off Pastor Long like water off a duck's back. In his view, Braden's labored and silly attempts to marry the current patriotic groundswell with Christmas were as a house built on sand, based as they were on a notion of that holiday as a celebration of peaceful love that crumbled under scrutiny. Accordingly, the annual Joy of Christmas program presented by FBCJ and juiced up this year with funds and equipment from Path to Judgment, was dedicated to illuminating the wondrous invasions through which God waged His perpetual war on evil.

FBCJ did not hire as many musicians as JUMC, but they made up for it with a newly purchased, superior sound and light system. After the spirited Broadway-style carol medley with which each show began (but now played with a few strings as well as winds, keyboard, and percussion), Pastor Long strolled out to welcome the audience. He was gratified to see that there were more visitors from further away than in previous years—a fact he attributed to the renown of Path to Judgment. As he began, he spread his arms wide, gesturing toward the white walls and stained-glass windows, now garlanded with holly, as if his fluttering hands could bring them to life.

"Welcome, friends, to the First Baptist Church of Jubilee's annual Joy of

Christmas program." He paused, dropping his arms. As he continued, his head jutted toward the audience, and he peered from side to side, surveying them. "I want to extend a special welcome to all those who've come from out of town, maybe out of the great state of Georgia—heck, maybe even out of the country—to celebrate this very special time of year with us here at FBCJ. You folks are extra near and dear to us because you've come from afar, like the Magi, and like those three Wise Men you've come bearing gifts.

"Now don't be alarmed," Pastor Long continued, thrusting out one arm toward the crowd as if he were stopping traffic. "I'm not puttin' my hand in your pocket. In my opinion, gold was not the most important gift the Wise Men brought our Savior—not by a long shot. Matter of fact, I don't believe this is in the Gospels, but some folks do say that the night *before* the Three Wise Men came with their gold, frankincense, and myrrh, the Three Wiser *Women* showed up, bringing diapers, formula, and a casserole" (here he paused to let the laughter subside). "The women arrived earlier because they had the sense to ask for directions" (more laughter).

"But seriously, friends, the most important gift the Wise Men brought is the most important gift all of us can bring—not just now, but *any* time we enter the House of the Lord to worship Jesus—and that is an open heart and a humble spirit. So we are grateful to everyone who brought these tonight, and most especially to those guests, those new friends, who made a special journey, maybe to an unfamiliar place, to give those gifts to Jesus through our worship in this Joy of Christmas program.

"And it's especially important, friends, that we open our hearts and humble our spirits at this time of the year, because as we all know, Christmas can make us feel almost like we're under attack—maybe even more so this Christmas season, when our Christian nation has so recently come under an actual attack.

"Folks, this feelin' of bein' attacked kinda puts me in mind of little Johnny when the supervisor of the Sunday school came to check what all the kids were learning. The supervisor comes into Johnny's class, and he says to Johnny, 'Tell me, son, who broke down the Wall of Jericho?' And right away Johnny says, 'I don't know, sir, but it sure wasn't me!'" (scattered laughter).

"The supervisor is a little surprised, so he turns to the teacher, and *she* jumps in and says, 'I can vouch for Johnny, sir. I've known him for years, and if he says he didn't do it, I believe him!'" (more laughter).

"By this time the supervisor is seriously upset by this obvious lack of biblical learning. So he goes to the deacon and tells him the whole story. 'I was shocked,' he says, 'that neither little Johnny nor his teacher could tell me who broke down the Wall of Jericho!'

"The deacon shrugs his shoulders and says, 'Listen, don't worry about it. I'll speak to Maintenance. They'll get three estimates and have that wall good as new in a week'" (general laughter).

"Now folks, that's a funny story, but it illustrates a powerful lesson about human nature, and that is, that when we're under pressure, we get defensive, and when we get defensive, what's the first thing we do? What's the first thing little Johnny said? 'It wasn't me. *I* didn't do it.' That's right: the first way we try to save ourselves when we come under attack is, denyin' responsibility.

"And what did the deacon say? 'I'll get Maintenance to take care of it. They'll fix the problem' My friends, that's the *second* thing it's in our nature to do, pass the buck. Maintenance'll fix it. If you think about it, that's really just another way to deny responsibility—just put it on the next guy. Let *him* take care of it.

"But friends, as I'm sure you've noticed, there's another side to the story here. Guess what? Nobody was being attacked. The supervisor wasn't accusing little Johnny of knocking down a wall. He wasn't complainin' to the deacon about the destruction of church property. He was just tryin' to bring the church closer to God by teachin' His word—namely the biblical story of Joshua and the Battle of Jericho. But he failed because everybody was too busy denyin' responsibility and passin' the buck to listen to God's word.

"Folks, I'm sure all of you remember that the Battle of Jericho was fought when the Israelites, led by Joshua, in*vad*ed the Promised Land, which had previously been occupied by the Canaanites, who the bible tells us were accursed. The Lord's people took over that land and just *filled* it with His mighty power, and folks, Joshua won the very first battle they fought in that holy invasion by blowin' his horn and causin' the Wall of Jericho to collapse.

"So now lemme ask you, friends, what if Joshua *hadn't* answered the call of the Lord to lead His people in that battle? What if he had just sorta hung fire, left his trumpet in its case? What if he'd refused responsibility—'What's it got to do with me?' like little Johnny; or 'Let some other guy fight this one,' like the deacon?" As he spoke, Pastor Long conjured these possibilities in the air with his hands. When he finished, he stood motionless for a beat, his hands suspended, while his audience wrestled with these troubling questions.

Then, dropping his arms to his sides the pastor bowed his head to the specters of defeat he had conjured up. But after a few seconds he suddenly fixed them once more with his piercing eagle eye. "Well folks, none of that happened, did it? The Lord knew how to pick His man.

"Now not to take anything away from Joshua—he was a great warrior. But think of the much *greater* invasion the Lord launched when he sent his only son, Jesus Christ, to fill the whole world with His saving power, so that now all of us—every Christian—can enter into that Promised Land and dwell there for eternity. Think of how Jesus knocks at the door of every heart"—here Pastor Long curled one large white hand into a fist and struck himself gently on the breastbone—"asking us to let Him in so that we can become His soldiers and go out spreading the good news of the Gospels far and wide in all the lands." Pastor Long outlined the globe with his hands. In the lights, the sweat on his bald dome gleamed like a beacon.

"My friends," he continued, in a comforting tone, "I know this time of year can be hard. But when we let Jesus Christ in*vade* our hearts, He lightens the burden, don't He? When we truly become filled with the saving power of Jesus, folks, we each and every one of us become a soldier in His invading army, spreading His Holy Spirit throughout the earth.

"And it is our hope and prayer here at FBCJ that when you leave here tonight you'll be able to say, 'Yes, Jesus, I want you to invade my heart. Make me a soldier in Your great army. Help me spread Your saving grace.'" He opened his arms again, his palms down as if calming troubled waters.

After allowing a moment for prayerful consideration, Pastor Long gently explained that if anyone felt moved to commit, or recommit, themselves to Jesus' saving mission that night, there were cards in the pew backs for them to fill out to get more information, as well as ministerial staff who would be happy to guide them in the way of the Lord.

XVI CHRISTMAS AND THE FLAME INSIDE

After the pastor's exit, Trip Holloway re-ascended the podium, and the concert continued with a sparkling opening number, "Hallelujah! Hosanna in the Highest!" Then the lights dimmed until the front of the church resembled a cocktail lounge, and the announcer (a DJ from WGNR, prerecorded) sonorously introduced Zach Finley, who would perform his own composition, "Light the Flame Inside."

Zach Finley was in his senior year at Jubilee's Munroe High School and stood out among the youth of FBCJ. From his mother, who was a Puerto Rican nurse, he had inherited an exotic, olive tint and melting brown eyes. From his father, a folk artist who had been discovered by an Atlanta gallery, gone to college with the help of a scholarship from a wealthy patron, and gotten a job teaching fine arts at NWGSU, Zach had inherited his curls and independent spirit. As he stepped on stage, picked up his guitar, and shook back his ringlets, a collective sigh, only partly suppressed, went through the female half of the audience, and Jim, sitting with Judy and Lynette, wished he had spent more time outdoors last summer during the landscaping, instead of teaching piano to his little monsters, as he fondly thought of them.

From his position in the choir loft, where he ran the sound and light system, Chase Moore experienced intense pangs of jealousy. He knew that Zach wouldn't even bother with church anymore if he weren't paid to provide music for the contemporary services. But the worst thing about Zach was Katie Engels's infatuation with the guy. Formerly, Chase had resented Zach's non-attendance at youth group, where he could really have boosted the female enthusiasm level, but now this seemed like a blessing.

There was not much for Chase to do after the lighting was set for Zach's solo, so as Zach went from soulfully lamenting a lonely, empty Christmas to triumphantly praising Jesus' miraculous power to "light the flame inside," Chase gradually let his mind drift from bitter comparisons between his loneliness and Zach's to that October night when he'd left the barn at Path to Judgment for a breath of fresh air and found Katie sobbing against a shadowy corner of the wall. He thought about how he'd put his arm around her without even thinking about it, about how soft her hair was and how it shimmered golden where the outside light hit it, and about how hard her frail, bony shoulders were shaking as she told him how she hated God.

And Chase, for once in his life, had done exactly the right thing. Drawing her close and leaning his head on hers he had said, "Well, that's pretty bad, but I think God can handle it, don't you?" And when she looked up, her smile through her tears was like a rainbow.

At last "Light the Flame Inside" came to an end with the keening notes of Zach's harmonica, yearning to spread the flame, and a few sighs from the audience. The announcer boomed out that "Christmas reminds us how even in hard times, God knows how to light His flame inside our hearts," and Chase altered the lighting as the children's choir gathered behind Zach for "The Christmas Shoes."

If there had been moist eyes and worshipfully parted lips when Zach sang of the flame of Jesus' love—"Touch me everywhere, make me burn for You"—these were as nothing compared to the audience's reaction to the tale of the boy trying to buy a pair of shoes for his dying mother. By the second time Zach sang the boy's speech about making his Mamma "beautiful" in case she "meets Jesus—tonight," open sobs were breaking out, and every young girl in the audience was brushing at least a few tears from her eyes. When the children took over the chorus, even grown men were wiping away the tears with one hand while they comforted weeping wives and girlfriends with the other. And by the time Macy Munroe's youngest, Tyler (age eight) came forward in his white robe and sang the line one last time, there wasn't a dry eye in the house, and old Mrs. Ruby Gilstrap hollered out, "Oh that poor little angel!" before dissolving into tears.

Lightening the mood and returning to the Gospel, Mercedes Finley, Zach's older sister and the ballet teacher at Superstarz! Academy, led on a troop of young ladies clad in long white tutus and red leotards emblazoned with silver Medieval crosses reminiscent of the Crusades. Just as angelic as Tyler, though faintly militant, they capered around in a tribute to the Nativity set to "The First Noël," to the great satisfaction of the audience. Jim Engels couldn't help but be proud of Katie's performance, despite his concerns over her persistent enthusiasm for the Baptist religion.

Chase had a lot to do in this number because the lighting went from single spots in the instrumental intro to a blaze of glory in the last chorus, but he found time to dwell on the swan-like necks—especially Katie's, under her gold bun—and extended legs, all so white, so delicate, and the tiny strip of leotard covering the space between their legs that could be glimpsed when they kicked sometimes before the veil of white tulle came down again, purity covering purity.

(But that was a lie, Chase thought, raging and remembering the chat rooms and the porn. They wanted it just as much as he did. And under the tulle and the little strips of fabric and the hot tights, each one—even Katie with her ethereal smile—was a velvety soft temptation to corruption and filth.)

After the announcer speculated briefly about Mary's state of mind on becoming the mother of the savior, Yolanda Tibbets appeared, sheathed in a red sequined gown that set off her dark skin, to sing "Mary Did You Know." Unlike Braden, Pastor Long had not courted and flattered her. That was not his style, and besides, he knew that no matter how much the higher-ups at the Southern Baptist Convention pontificated about forging a bond with African American National Baptist Convention churches, none of that made any never-mind to Yolanda, who would never forgive FBCJ for refusing to allow her father and Althea to get married in the sanctuary under Pastor Long's predecessor, back in the late '80s. So he had merely swallowed his indignation at the high figure she set for her performance (it was twice as high as the one she accepted from Braden, but Pastor Long would have hired her even if he had known) and authorized Trip to comply with all her terms—a two-page spread on the role of Henderson's BBQ in "meeting all your holiday entertaining needs" was included in the deal.

He did not regret his decision. Yolanda's sultry tones seemed to the pastor to be carrying the whole tragic history of her race in a way that sent shivers up the spine as she sang the wondrous, forlorn, yet ultimately triumphant story of the mother of a baby who was also the savior of the world. Behind her on a newly purchased screen, the Jesus of *The Jesus Film* looked out with soulful, earnest eyes set in a pale face framed with light brown hair while he performed miracles and was persecuted. Pastor Long was pleased to see that Associate Pastor Randle had carefully integrated the clips with the song so that as miracles were mentioned Jesus worked them on the screen. Yolanda's voice gained in power as it told of Jesus' greatness, so that when the choir came in after "when you kiss your little baby, you kiss the face of God," her improvised "oo-oo-oo-oo" floated effortlessly over them, full of wonder and grief as the scenes of Jesus' suffering and crucifixion appeared. It was a *tour de force* whose impact could be measured by the unusual stillness, bursting into prolonged applause, at its close.

"Angels We have Heard on High" finished off the first half, with the sopranos stronger than usual on the "*Gloria in excelsis deo*," as if inspired.

#

The Trans-Siberian Orchestra's powerfully aggressive version of "The Carol of the Bells" served as the entr'acte. Following it, the lights dimmed, and the female portion of the youth choir entered from the rear, clad in modest but filmy nightgown-like robes, each holding a candle. To a doctored "Hark! The Herald Angels Sing," they proclaimed that Jesus sang in their hearts "at this special time—each year."

They were radiant, and Chase cynically reflected that Zach's performance probably had a greater influence over their hearts than Jesus. Katie had her hair down now, Chase noticed, and he thought with renewed rage about the supposed purity under the nightgowns and the "special night" that even the virginal Mary must have had when the Holy Ghost came upon her—maybe it was blasphemous, but he couldn't help trying to picture to himself what she felt in that moment. Then he thought of his own Christmas nights and how unspecial it was to watch some drively "special" in his brother-in-law's den, and how Hannah Grace never paid any mind to him, but Katie was not like that. She was truly special—thoughtful, and as pure as it was possible for a mere mortal to be.

As they continued to sing, his mind drifted, conjuring up an ultimately special night where he lay paralyzed, enchanted, and young female figures, aching with their burdens of purity, approached, opened their filmy white robes, and pressed themselves against him, forcing their budding breasts into his mouth, making him suck the nipples to a deep, ruby red like ripened fruit . . .

He nearly missed his cue at the end of the song. The lights had to go to red, with a spotlight on Destiny Jenkins, whose father was the manager down at the Piggly Wiggly. Destiny was nine, and she had on a red satin party dress with puffy sleeves and a green ribbon in her long black hair. Nothing about Destiny yet evoked Chase's obsession with the secret fires burning in young teenage girls, and he was able to concentrate better as she sang "Happy Birthday Jesus." He knew Trip was mouthing the words to her and smiling encouragement. When she got to "but the real gift is you," Chase hoped and prayed along with Trip that she would make it up to the "you" note OK this time, and he shared Trip's disappointment as the note rang out slightly flat.

XVII HANDSOME RANSOM AND THE SLIPPERY SLOPE

After the choir had finished their own full-throated outpouring of birthday wishes and the applause and murmurs of "Wasn't she *precious*?" and "Bless her heart" had stilled, there was a hush as Pastor Long strode on stage again.

"Wasn't that wonderful, my friends?" he began. "I know I say it every year, but our Joy of Christmas program really does seem to just get better and better, don't it?" (scattered applause). "In fact, I truly believe, folks, that this year, with our new sound and light system, run by our youth pastor, Chase Moore, and longtime FBCJ member, Mike Hardacre—thanks, guys" —he waved to Chase and Mike in the choir loft, and there was again scattered applause—"I truly believe this *is* the best Joy of Christmas program we've ever had." This time the applause was longer, and a couple of amens rang out.

"While I'm at it, I want to thank our music minister, Dr. Trip Holloway— " Trip bowed to the applause—"and our organist, the lovely Miss Marie Simms—that sexagenarian stood and bowed from her place behind the seated choir. "And I want to thank our choir and our orchestra, and our ushers—you know it takes a lot of people to put this on, my friends, and we are so very blessed to have so many talented and dedicated people in the Jubilee community who have come together to make this celebration so very special.

"Finally, I want to thank my lovely bride, Melanie, my better half for goin' on eighteen years." Pastor Long graciously extended an arm toward her place in the choir, and she rose and bowed with her customary sweet smile.

"Yes, friends, we've come together tonight to enjoy the efforts of all these wonderfully talented and dedicated people, and to celebrate the birth of our Lord, Jesus Christ. But if you recall, I said earlier that Christmas is not just a celebration but an in*va*sion. Now folks, I know that when we think of invasions, we don't think of good things. We don't like it, for example, when we have to undergo an in*va*sive medical procedure. And of course we're all aware that our military has launched a dangerous invasion into Afghanistan. But hold on a minute and let's just think on that for a bit. Our military launched that invasion because we were *attacked*. And what about that medical procedure? Yes, friends, that too is a response to an attack—an attack on our bodies by illness. And the invasion is looking to remove the problem and make us whole again, isn't it, my friends?"

Chase put the picture of Mike Abbott in his firefighter's uniform up on the screen behind the minister. Mike was darker than his brother Johnny, so that his happy eyes and proud smile gleamed out all the brighter under his firefighter's hat. At the bottom of the picture, spelled out in white letters, were his name, "Michael Ransom Abbott," followed by "Sept. 13, 1972-Nov. 2, 2002."

A hushed murmur of recognition went through the audience. Several heads turned to look at Althea and her family, who stood out against the sea of white faces. Yolanda, who had joined Althea, Johnny, and her father in the pews, put her arm around her stepmother, who got a lace-trimmed white hankie out of her purse and blew her nose audibly.

"My friends," resumed Pastor Long, after the audience had gotten a grip on themselves again, "those of you who have attended our Christmas program before will remember that at this time in the evening we customarily pay tribute to a Christian hero. Someone who embodies the triumph of faith in Jesus Christ over earthly struggles, and beyond that, someone who, through their faith, has made spiritual, and often material, contributions to all our lives.

"Now often, my friends, when it comes time to choose who we're gonna talk about, Pastor Randle and I have to think long and hard about it, and I'm not gonna lie to you, we sometimes even get to fussin'. But this past November 2nd, when we got the sad news that Mike Ransom Abbott—'Handsome Ransom,' as he was known to his many friends—had passed, Pastor Randle and I happened to meet up in the hallway the next morning, and folks, it was like God was just speakin' through us. We didn't even greet each other first. There was no 'Good mornin', how ya doin'?'—none of that. No, friends, at the very same time we both said to each other, 'Did you hear about Mike Abbott?' And then, again together, in absolute synchronicity, we both started talkin' about what a great Christian he was, and how fitting it would be to pay tribute to him at this time." Pastor Long's capacious hands joined to illustrate the synchronicity he described, and he bowed his head in preparation for his story.

Raising it again and gazing over the audience like an eagle on the hunt, he began. "Friends, as many of you know, at one time in his life, Handsome

Ransom was nobody's idea of a hero. His older brother, Jubilee's own Councilman Johnny Abbott" (Pastor Long gestured toward where Johnny sat in the audience) "—*he* was the straight arrow, the achieving go-getter, but for whatever reason things just didn't come easy to young Mike. After his father, Johnny Senior, passed when Mike was just fifteen years old, he fell in with a bad crowd—yes, folks, it is possible to do that, even in Jubilee—and began cuttin' school.

"Now friends, as you all know, once you give in to sin and begin down that slippery slope, things can get a whole lot worse in a hurry. Mike turned away from his church, his old friends, his loving home and family. He dropped out of school altogether, and it wasn't long before he was arrested for selling marijuana." Pastor Long paused for the audience to sigh and shake their heads over this inevitability. Necks craned for a view of the family who had suffered through it all. Those who paid good money to send their kids to the mostly white Jubilee Christian Academy inwardly patted themselves on the back.

"Now at the time, as some of you remember, I was just startin' out as Associate Pastor here at FBCJ. And one of my jobs was to oversee and promote Outreach and Missions. These days, I've mostly had to take off that particular hat and hand it to my associate and close personal friend, Pastor Randle" (Pastor Long gestured to where Jeff Randle sat with his family in one of the front pews). "But, friends, there is one mission I was involved in that I just can't give up, no matter how many calls I have on my time, and that is the one inspired by Chuck Colson's Prison Fellowship ministries." The picture of Mike Abbott disappeared as Chase put up a picture of Pastor Long and Chuck Colson smiling at the camera together.

"Now friends, as many of you know, Charles Colson had his own troubles with the law at one time. Some of you will remember he was caught up in the Watergate scandal, and was actually sent to prison for his loyalty to President Nixon in that affair. But guess what, friends? This humbling experience was the best thing that could have happened to him. Why? Because only when he saw how empty his worldly career was could he make room for Jesus Christ to in*vade* his life. And not only did he give *his* life over to our Lord; he vowed to dedicate himself to prison ministry so as to win over as many *others* to Jesus as he could. So his friendship and inspiring example is one reason why I can't give up my work with our own church's ministry to help at-risk youth and those tryin' to reintegrate themselves into society.

"But Mike Abbott gave me a reason, too. Folks, when I learned that Mike was in juvenile detention, the Lord just seemed to speak to me, because I knew in my heart that my experience with Prison Fellowship Ministries made me uniquely situated to reach out to this young man, and because I knew of his fine family and all they had done for the community, I felt sure that he *could* be reached, and that not reaching him would be a needless tragedy.

"So I called up his family's pastor at the time, the late Reverend Alvin Thornberry, who many of you will remember was Pastor over at Mount Zion Baptist for some thirty-five years. Fortunately he had also been involved in prison work, so he called up the family, and I remember they were pretty surprised, but they agreed to us coming over together to pray on the situation, which we did, and in the end they were one hundred percent supportive of FBCJ Missions reaching out to Mike.

"Now keep in mind, folks, at this time Handsome Ransom was known to boast that he didn't have any use for church or school or anybody. He was tough, and he was gonna go it alone, come hell or high water. But by that time, I had some experience in prison outreach, and I wasn't intimidated by attitude. No, I knew, my friends, that at the bottom of Handsome Ransom's attitude was fear, and darkness, and hopelessness.

"So I didn't take what you might call the direct approach. No, I just went in to his room one day, and I put a piece of paper and a pencil down in front of him, and I gave him a very simple assignment, my friends. I asked him to write down his goals for next year, for five years from now, and yes, even a decade down the road.

"And do you know that young man, Handsome Ransom, who just moments ago had been all ready to fight me and kick me out of his room—he just looked at me like I was from Mars or something? Because the sad fact is, folks, as he told me later, Handsome Ransom didn't have any goals, apart from gettin' high every day."

Chase put up a picture of a smiling Handsome Ransom in a cap and gown, shaking hands with a younger Pastor Long in a high-school gym. "My friends, from that day forward everything started looking up for Mike Abbott. In fact, it wasn't very long after I in*vad*ed his room that day before Mike began to feel that he was being invaded by something else, something way bigger'n he'd bargained for. Yes, friends, before he was even out of detention, Michael Abbott allowed himself to be invaded by our Lord Jesus Christ when he accepted Him as his personal savior and was baptized by Pastor Thornberry in the detention center chapel, with friends and family looking on." Chase put up a picture of a wet, smiling Mike in a baptismal font with the elderly Pastor Thornberry."

XVIII MIKE ABBOTT, HERO

"Well, friends," Pastor Long continued, "young Mike turned eighteen and got a clean record, but more importantly, he was right with the Lord. He earned his GED and got an associates degree from Butler County Community College, but he also wanted to give back, and so he remained active in his church, often attending religious conferences and retreats.

"And at one of these retreats, he met his wife, a lovely young Christian woman by the name of Tameka Foster. Now I was privileged to meet Tameka, and I can tell you, she isn't one to sit around and let the moss grow on her. Matter of fact, Tameka was studying to be a chef and working in New York City at a fancy restaurant, which meant Mike had to relocate if he didn't wanna let this one get away.

"Well of course Mike did move to New York City, and he married the lovely Tameka, and became a firefighter, and the rest, as they say, is history. Most of that history we all know only too well, don't we, friends? We all know how the terrorists *attacked* our soil and flew their planes into the towers and the Pentagon" (Chase put up the iconic picture of the World Trade Center with thick black smoke billowing around the towers, eliciting murmurs of recognition from the crowd).

"I think we can picture—can't we, folks?—the firefighters battling the fierce flames, doing their heroic best as bodies began to fall out of the sky" (Chase put up a picture of firefighters amidst the flames). "But what we don't know are all the stories within the story of that day—all the little acts of kindness and heroic sacrifice that we Americans are known for but that oftentimes don't make the evening news. And one of those stories is Mike's.

"Recollect, friends, that for some time after the news came that the second tower, the South Tower, had been hit, our brave first responders were still climbing up the North Tower, assisting and rescuing people wherever they could. Keep in mind, there were no elevators and often no lights except whatever they had brought with them.

"Then came the terrible news that the North Tower was going to collapse. Everyone had to get out, and the firefighters had to help, and try and get out themselves. Now by this time Mike Abbott had climbed up to the twenty-second floor." Pastor Long paused to let this sink in. "That's a long way down, folks. It's a long way, and there were a lot of people to help.

"Yes, a *lot* of people, so it's understandable that many of them—yes, even Mike's fellow firefighters—passed by the overweight gentleman who was sitting on the stairs around the eighteenth floor because he had hurt his ankle. It's understandable, my friends, because after all, they had in*vad*ed the North Tower to save as many lives as possible, and no doubt they calculated that if they helped that one man, there would be many other people they couldn't help.

"But my friends, that's the thing about the Holy Spirit of our Lord Jesus Christ. *It just don't calculate.* No, folks, *Jesus* is all about the *heart.* And so it was a mark of how fully Mike had been in*vad*ed and just—just taken *over* by the Holy Spirit that, as he told it to me, he didn't even stop to think when he saw that man on the stairs and everyone rushing past him just as fast as they could. No, folks, much like the good Samaritan of the bible, Mike simply went over to the man, got him on his feet, and began helping him down those stairs. Never mind that the clock was ticking and they very well might not make it out in time. All those kind of concerns had just been *driven out* by Jesus' loving kindness.

"And sure enough, Mike saved that man's life and his own as well. The power of Jesus was that strong in him, my friends." Pastor Long paused. The audience sat quiet and rapt, all trying to believe that they, too, would have stopped and helped.

Taking a deep breath, Pastor Long resumed. "Tragically, Mike paid the ultimate price for his heroic actions that day. You see, his lungs were damaged from the smoke and the dust, and he was never fully able to recover." Althea sniffled loudly here, and several startled heads turned in her direction. They had forgotten for a moment that Mike Abbott was a real person who had once lived in their town. Chase put up the first portrait of Mike in his firefighter's uniform again. "Mike developed cancer, and just this past November, as you can see, he went to be with the Lord." Pastor Long paused again, allowing for a respectful silence. Then, with another audible breath, he resumed.

"As you leave here tonight, friends, I hope and pray that your souls have been in*vad*ed by the life of Michael Ransom Abbott. And if they have, I think you'll find yourself thinking of Christmas a whole lot differently maybe than you've ever thought of it before. Because Mike Abbott isn't the only person who's been invaded by the powerful spirit of our Lord Jesus Christ. Oh no. Jesus is the light of the *world*, my friends.

"Yes, folks, if you think about it, Christmas is really a celebration of God's wonderful, miraculous in*va*sion of our sinful world. And I want to propose to each of you that you open yourselves heart and soul to that invasion, and that you *celebrate* the power of Jesus to root out evil by invading our lives and our world with the mighty Christian spirit. Because that, my friends, is the true reason for the season."

Pastor Long reported that in 2001 nineteen people had made a decision to give their lives over to Jesus after the Joy of Christmas Program. He reminded them that anyone who was even considering a decision to let Jesus invade their lives this year should fill out one of the cards in the pew backs and put them in the ushers' baskets on their way out, and they could also get more information from Associate Pastor Randle and his assistants in the church library after the concert. Then Pastor Long asked them all to pray the sinner's prayer with him—"All eyes closed, every head bowed"—and on everyone's behalf he acknowledged that he was a sinner and asked Jesus to "invade my life and destroy all worldly evil."

XIX A STRANGE WAY TO SAVE THE WORLD

After a pause while Pastor Long left the stage, the announcer boomed out, "The heavens and the earth, all the wonders of creation, bear witness to the awesome power of our living God," while Chase put up a slideshow of stars and planets, mountains and oceans. The choir sang Third Day's "God of Wonders," and some of the other men besides Zach got solos. On the chorus the choir began to sway back and forth to the rhythm of "You are ho—ly, You are ho—ly," and some parts of the audience swayed too.

Then the announcer boomed out John 3:16, "For God so loved the world that He gave His one and only Son that whoever believes in Him shall not perish but have eternal life," adding, "Some might say this was a strange way to save the world." 4Him's "A Strange Way to Save the World" followed, with Zach soloing on the opening verses, accompanied by a montage slideshow highlighting the humbleness of Jesus' birth and earthly family by juxtaposing them with angels, heavenly rays of light, and shepherd and magi worship.

Davis McGraw then stepped forward for his annual "O Holy Night." He was a young lawyer just starting out, a former Marine, veteran of the First Gulf War, and not exactly handsome, but rugged in a way that made married women wish their husbands went to the gym more often. Jim recognized this quality, though McGraw was not his type—he liked a certain boyishness. Besides his barrel-chested vigor, the man had a surprising, powerful tenor voice. His climactic "O ni-ight—di*vi*-i-i-ine!" was effortless, and while he sang it his whole well-built body seemed to strain upwards, as though he might be raptured away by the spotlight at any moment.

As the resounding applause died down, Chase turned on the white lights wrapped around a large wooden cross to one side of the choir, and they sang "Start at the Manger." As the song built, the men came in, and then the orchestra crescendoed, with not quite enough strings but a good trumpet solo from Trent Brown, the band teacher over at Munroe High. Some of the fathers in the audience were distracted when the song asked auditors to imagine they owned "the wealth of the world," but by the end all were moved by the thought of the humble path of duty from manger to cross that all must follow to gain salvation and eternal glory.

The "Hallelujah Chorus" concluded the program, and, as at FUMC, everyone who could stand jumped up. Those who knew the story of King George at the first performance felt vaguely royal, but even those who only stood because everyone else did felt it was an appropriate expression of upliftedness.

The choirs and soloists all bowed, with the dancers who weren't in any choirs, and Trip had the orchestra stand up while he bowed. Then, as instructed, he dismissed the audience. "We here at First Baptist of Jubilee want to thank y'all for coming. We ask that you let the spirit of our Lord Jesus Christ invade your hearts and your homes this Christmas season. God bless you and keep you! Good night!"

As he waved and smiled his jolly smile, many waved back, yelling out, "Merry Christmas, Trip!" "Great show tonight!" "Just gets better every year!" and the like.

#

Indeed the program was an unparalleled success, both spiritually and tactically. Fully twenty-three souls accepted Jesus as a result of it, and at least twelve mothers received a pretty pair of shoes from their children that Christmas. It was generally conceded, among those of whatever faith who had attended both concerts, that although the Methodist Christmas Concert had been "great fun," FBCJ's Living Christmas was more spiritually enriching. It was good to have the firm ground of Pastor Long's Christian teachings to stand on when considering what course America should take in regard to Iraq. Pleasure was all very well, in its way, as Clayton Briggs opined to Officer Dillingham when the latter stopped in for a new washer to put on the kitchen sink, but there wouldn't be a whole lot of pleasure if Saddam Hussein and the terrorists were allowed to just attack the American way of life whenever they wanted, simply to gratify their lust for virgins in the hereafter. Marvin Patterson, who was purchasing materials to help Rita Hill install a new barre at Superstarz! Academy, was forced to agree.

There seemed little doubt that Saddam had WMDs, and the only way to stop him from pointing them in America's direction was a righteous invasion like what Pastor Long had talked about. Delia Rosenbaum and her gang of harpies from over at the university could dress up in black and stand on the corner of Jubilee Square "witnessing" all they wanted. That wasn't gonna change a single solitary thing.

#

Braden felt some pressure. Officially, everyone at JUMC agreed that Christmas was not an appropriate time for serious military matters, but everyone also knew that Pastor Long had fundamentally influenced the town's thinking about war. Of course, only rude frat boys from over at the university and eccentrics like Clint Farrow would yell out, "Nuke 'em all, and let Allah sort 'em out!"—and then only when provoked, as when driving by Delia and her witnessing crew. But now when politer people spoke of the possibility of invading Iraq, they did so with no hesitation—with pride, even—confident in their good intentions. They burned to rescue the oppressed Muslims in Iraq, just as Mike Abbott had rescued the fat man on the stairs of the North Tower.

Even Jim Engels, who grew gloomy at the very sight of the church on the other side of the square, seemed to rub Braden's face in its triumph, shaking his head when the "invasion sermon" was mentioned and growling, "He sure has a way with words, that man."

Outwardly, Braden remained unflappable. He resolved to take the high road at Easter, but promised a full-scale celebration of militant Christian patriotism for the Fourth of July. (But how could he plan, he thought, slightly panicked, when no one had any idea when the war would be or how long it would last?)

#

Then came the invasion, the godlike shock and awe, the endless treks through the desert filmed live by bravely embedded reporters. Resentment against French nonparticipation became a popular new way to demonstrate patriotism. No one had ever really liked the French anyway, with their stuck-up ways, their fancy food, their impossible language, their inability to fight their own battles. Now several of the restaurants around town offered "freedom fries" on their menu, and at the end of the year the high school had to let one of its French teachers go because so few students signed up to study the language.

While the invasion unfolded on TV and enlivened the spirits of Jubileeans, the tulip trees and crabapples and redbuds were giving way to a riot of azaleas. Even Mother Nature seemed to proclaim the superiority of this blessed land over the barren monotony of the one being saved.

XX PASTORAL INTERLUDE

Katie Engels and her friends Jenna Whitfield and Hannah Grace Dillingham were blossoming, too. Their legs were longer, their breasts more developed. They bubbled with enthusiasm over everything in their own world and were inexpressibly bored with everything outside it. They became self-conscious. They knew that when the boys at the junior high put each other in headlocks it was to impress them, so they supremely ignored such behavior. They knew that when the Dillinghams took them out to Sam's Pizza for Hannah Grace's birthday, T. J. only ordered a salad because Katie did—and they fell over laughing about this in private while priding themselves on their maturity for not taunting him publicly.

They felt they had no power over Zach—who, it was rumored, only saw college women—and worshipped him accordingly. And Hannah and Jenna, more than suspecting Chase's wandering eyes and eager touch, scorned him.

"You know how Uncle Chase always gives you those *looong* hugs?" Hannah Grace asked rhetorically, as they sat eating their lunch and surveying their domain at the top of a small hill outside the junior high.

"So?" Katie shrugged. Jenna and Hannah Grace always wanted to make a big deal out of things. Secretly she thought it was kind of sweet that Chase couldn't conceal his susceptibility. She also believed it was all mixed up with how seriously he took his job and how much he really did care about everyone in youth group.

Jenna, however, grew instantly animated. "I know, right? It's not like I'm even related to him or anything."

Hannah Grace shivered histrionically. "It's worse *because* I'm related. Gives me the creeps."

"And he's a pastor, too," Jenna said. The girls were silent for a moment, contemplating the delicious horror of a pastor unable to control his weakness for them.

Katie was anxious to dispel it. "But it's not like he's ever *done* anything, you know—wrong? Has he?"

"I'd like to see him try," said Jenna, crumpling her lunch bag.

Katie did not openly disagree with her friends when they talked about what a creepy perv Pastor Moore was, but privately she believed they just didn't understand him. Ever since that night outside the barn at Path to Judgment when she had been all freaked out and he had talked to her and put his arm around her, she sensed that they had a special connection with each other. Like, she hadn't had to explain to him *why* she was feeling like she hated God. He just knew because he had his own struggles, Katie thought. She could see it in his eyes when he gently pushed her hair back and asked her if she believed she was made in God's image and explained to her how God was inside of us, so hating God was like hating yourself—and hating yourself was like hating God.

It was almost like there was a flicker of doubt there, and as he went on talking about how hard it could be to find God and trust in Him and how easy it was to want to blame Him for all our sinfulness and the pain it brought, Katie knew he was not just giving her some canned message, but actually a coded version of his own spiritual journey. She felt that, in a different way from Zach, Pastor Moore was deep and mysterious.

And unlike Zach, Pastor Moore took her seriously and didn't treat her like a child. She didn't deny what her friends said about his lingering touch or close hugs, or the way he seemed to be undressing girls with his eyes. But she felt that it was all part of his painful, romantic struggle to find God in everyone, most of all in himself. And she believed that when he looked at her with his penetrating gaze or touched her as he talked to her about God, it was because he knew she was different, more introspective, better able to understand things than the others.

Because she *had* understood. She understood from what he had said and the way he had said it, looking straight into her eyes, that all the changes that made her uncomfortable—the new things her body was and did, the new way guys looked at her, the new things she thought about her parents, her friends, God—everything, really—all this was not, as she had thought at first, something to fear, but a powerful force to own, embrace and use wisely—a godly force, in fact.

This realization had changed Katie's life. She intuited the sterility of her parents' marriage and associated it with their religion, which she viewed as formulaic, superficial, and childish, in contrast with the Baptists' emphasis on sin and seeking a deep spiritual connection with God. As she began to feel she had established this connection, she moved through life with increased confidence in her understanding of God's divine power in her, and this made her old friends seem silly to her at the same time that it attracted the positive attention of Jenna and Hannah Grace. Like Katie, they were sure of themselves, though their security came from being popular and admired. They knew that Katie's self-possessed beauty would elevate them as a group and sensed that her introspection made her nonthreatening, even somewhat passive, in their hands. As yet she had no inkling of this, however, and simply enjoyed being with others who seemed strong and passionate like herself.

#

Chase disregarded the scorn of Jenna and Hannah Grace but bore Katie's tantalizing crush like a hair shirt. He rigidly scheduled his days, working himself into exhausted bouts of illness, and volunteered to lead an arduous mission to Uganda in the summer, reasoning that few parents would allow their young teenage daughters to go and that the physically exhausting hard labor entailed in supplying village infrastructure would keep him out of trouble.

But still, at the lonely end of many days there was the magic window of his computer offering freedom and every imaginable debauchery—including several he would never have imagined on his own. He liked to watch free clips—he was leery of giving his information to a website and vaguely felt it was more sinful to pay—and his favorite kind of porn was hentai. First of all, it wasn't real. In fact, sitting down to it reminded him of getting up and watching Saturday morning cartoons in his pajamas. Then, too, the girls always looked very young and spoke in high, squeaky voices, and the ordinary guys (not the repulsive brute characters) were like Chase himself—just well-intentioned, slightly geeky guys. They showed the girls what they'd always wanted and needed, had they only known, but instead of being reviled for this, as Chase knew he would be, they became powerful, confident studs.

Even better, because further removed from reality, were the tentacled monsters. Ordinarily Chase did not watch the same clips over and over. They lost their freshness. But there was one that he enjoyed so much he would often rehearse it dreamily during the day, sometimes in an aimless, drifting way that wasn't even particularly sexual.

The young girl was sunbathing provocatively on a dock. The background was all simple, bright colors, but the girl was not noticing the magical scene. She seemed completely absorbed—whether innocently or not was impossible to tell—in laying herself out.

Then, out of the sea, the tentacles came slithering, at first so gently that the girl, betraying her true, sensual nature, merely stirred under their caress, parting her lips. Encouraged, the tentacles grew bolder, snaking up between her legs and wreathing over her small, tender breasts. By the time she became alarmed, it was too late. She tried to sit up but was pulled back down. She made the mistake of opening her mouth wide to cry out—a tentacle went in, turning her protest to a gagged whimper. Multiplying, some tentacles twined round her wrists, holding them away from her body, while others plucked off her bikini top and applied suckers to her nipples, turning them red and erect as she moaned in pleasured protest.

She arched her back—trying to get away or participating, who could tell?—and more tentacles pulled off her suit bottom. Then, as she twisted, they delicately pulled her labia apart, finally applying a merciless sucker to the little pink clit. Her moans increasing in volume, she was penetrated and fucked willy-nilly by a large thick tentacle, then flipped like a pancake and suspended while the tentacles pulled apart her ass cheeks and invaded her delicate asterisk asshole.

Chase's favorite part was the end, when the tentacles, still inside her, picked her up and bore her off into the sunset. She didn't seem to be struggling anymore, but to be fully the creature's creature, with no existence of her own at all. After she and the monster had disappeared into the sea near the horizon, the sun continued to set for a second or two. A bird flipped across the screen with a piercing cry, and the water lapped peacefully at the dock as though nothing could ever disturb the idyllic scene.

XXI ANGELS

At Easter, the war in Iraq going well, both churches tacitly agreed to emphasize the spiritual importance of the holiday, but the spirit of competition was not completely dispelled among their respective factions, who couldn't help but note the effects on morale of these purportedly peaceable endeavors.

On Maundy Thursday FBCJ held a Tenebrae service at which they presented an unobjectionable cantata by a contemporary Christian composer who ably cobbled together the milder aspects of Schubert, Mendelssohn, and—at moments of high drama—Brahms. This was fairly well attended by middle-aged empty nesters and the elderly, many of whom were moved to tears by Alessandro Trentini's violin solo in the *Agnus Dei* movement.

On Good Friday, Alessandro was at work at JUMC, which held a Grief Service featuring Barber's *Adagio for Strings*. This was rather sparsely attended. Everyone agreed that the music was magnificent, though, and Cyrus Buell gave a good sermon, based on Ecclesiastes 3, about allowing a time for grief. Marvin Patterson, for one, declared that he felt like a new man afterwards. Saturday morning he went over to Waterman's Jewelers to pick out an engagement ring for Rita Hill.

Easter morning began with JUMC's Sunrise Service at Braxton Park. Reverend Hollifield released brilliantly colored butterflies that flew east into the muted reds and oranges of the rising sun. Fortunately the wind was blowing west to east as well. The Braxton Foundation and other organizations had been making progress in cleaning up Jubilee Creek, which ran through the east side of the park, but drought, combined with the quarry's demands on local aquifers, had reduced the stream's water level, concentrating levels of smelly pollutants and exposing a stagnant, multi-colored oily sludge in the stream bed. As this was screened from view and not wafted toward the congregation, however, the event was an uplifting success. Reverend Hollifield's delivery—rising in pitch before the pauses, emphasizing the next word on a still higher pinnacle, then plunging down to trail off almost in a sigh—was dramatic, yet comforting as a well-known song. When he evoked his dear mother sitting up in her hospital bed to greet the "bright angels—*on* the other side," all eyes turned towards the creek, as though the butterflies, transmuted into angels, might be hovering there.

At 10 a.m., back at the church, Reverend Hollifield gave his main sermon, which included not only the story of his mother, but an affecting anecdote concerning a little girl with cancer who brought her feuding parents together over her deathbed.

"And suddenly Anna Beth—*sat* up, and for the first time, almost, since her illness, her parents—*saw* her smile, and O Lord, it was radiant. . . . And Anna Beth cried out, she said—'Mamma, Daddy—I *see* them! I see Nanna. I see Pop Pop!' And she pointed—*at* the wall. She said, 'Oh, it's so beautiful—*on* the other side. . . .'" Reverend Hollifield pointed too, seemingly transfixed.

"But then suddenly Anna Beth, *fell* back." The reverend's hand dropped heavily to his side, and he slumped. "And when her parents had wiped the tears—*from* their eyes, they saw—they saw that little Anna Beth—*was* crying.

"And her mother asked her, 'Anna Beth—*why* are you crying?'

Reverend Hollified straightened up, just as Anna Beth would, gathering strength. "And Anna Beth answered, she said, 'I'm crying for you, Mamma, and I'm crying for you too, Daddy,' and her parents said—*through* their tears, 'But why, honey? We're gonna be there one day. We're gonna see you.'" The minister clasped his hands together and wrung them as the parents would have done, then let go and opened his arms helplessly.

"But Anna Beth—*shook* her head—she was getting weaker now—she said, 'I'm afraid I—*won't* see you, though, because you see, you're not—*Chris*tians.'

"Her parents hurried to reassure her. 'But Anna Beth, honey, we *are* Christian. Haven't you gone to church with us every Sunday?'

"And Anna Beth said, 'Oh yes—*I* have. And I heard the minister say—"*Love* one another."'

"And Anna Beth's mother said, '*Yes*, Anna Beth. So you know—we *are* Christians.'

"But Anna Beth shook her head—she said, 'But Mamma and Daddy, *you* only love one another—*on* Sunday.'" A murmur of subdued laughter rippled through the sanctuary. Reverend Hollifield looked out at them with ineffable sadness.

"Right then and there," he continued, "Anna Beth's parents looked across her hospital bed—at *each* other—really looked, for the first time in, *many* months—and they realized that our of the mouths of babes had come—*great* wisdom. And they took hold of each other's hands across little Anna Beth's—*hospital* bed, and she put her weak little hand—*on* theirs and witnessed as they solemnly swore to be Christians for the—*whole* week from here on out.

"And when they had sworn, little Anna Beth—*fell* back with—with just the—*hap*piest smile, *and* Jesus took her." Reverend Hollifield waited for a moment in silence, then returned to earthly matters.

"Now, I wish I could tell you that from that moment Anna Beth's parents were—*re*united, but unfortunately things don't always work out right in our imperfect—*earth*ly world. Too much damage had been done, and in the end they did—*get* divorced. But I can tell you that they also—*kept* their promise to Anna Beth. From that moment on they put aside their petty squabbles. They learned to love and respect one another—*as* Christians. Anna Beth's father appreciated what a good mother—*she* was, to his children. And she realized that—for *all* his faults, he was a caring, *hard*-working Dad, and she made every effort to include him in their surviving children's lives—*as* they grew up. And so, thanks to—*little* Anna Beth, the whole family learned—*to* love each other, and to truly be—*Chris*tian, *every* day of the week."

Reverend Hollifield paused to let his lesson sink in. Rita Hill sighed sentimentally and squeezed Marvin Patterson's hand. Fortunately, neither of the children from her first marriage had died and there had been no children from her second. She doubted that she would have been able to respect her first husband, a pot-smoking layabout, even if little Ashley or Christopher had wasted away before their eyes, As for Scott, her second husband, an engineering professor over at the university, she had loathed him implacably from the moment she had walked in on him screwing his pretty Chinese grad student. But all that was over and done with, and now that the pot smoker was in rehab (again) for his pain killer addiction and the professor had moved onward and upward to Auburn University, and she had Marvin, she forgave them with true Christian spirit.

Marvin squeezed her hand back. His was a little sweaty. He was thinking of the ring he had bought and how Linda had said she wanted him to be happy, so in a way he was respecting her memory by proposing to Rita, though he was quite sure Linda would have thought Rita was "loud," by which Linda would have meant low class. With his other hand Marvin brushed away a tear at the thought of Linda in her hospital deathbed, her body shriveled, her hair stubbly from chemo, telling him to be happy yet comforted by his misery.

Reverend Hollifield wound up his sermon by exhorting them all to be "true Christians—*every* day," and they went home to Easter dinner feeling cleansed and newly empowered to fight their own sinfulness.

XXII PROSTITUTES

Like JUMC, FBCJ had an early service, but theirs was baptismal. In the distant past, Jubilee Creek had been used for this, but not in living memory. This was the first year in which the Whitfields' farm was used. Branch Creek, a healthy-sized tributary of the Jubilee waterway, ran through the Whitfields' land, and at 9 a.m. about fifty people had gathered at a clear, wide place known as "the swimmin' hole." These included a portion of the choir who, led by Trip Holloway, sang old-timey hymns like "Shall We Gather at the River." Pastor Randle preached briefly about the resurrection and the need to accept Jesus in order to follow Him to heaven, and then he went and stood in his white robe in the middle of the stream where the water was almost four feet deep, and eleven people were baptized for the first time and several others baptized again, either because they had transferred from another faith or because they felt a deep-seated need to recommit their lives to Christ.

After warm clothes and coffee and hot chocolate in the barn, some went home to brunch and others, including Pastor Randle and the choir, went to the church, where Pastor Long preached a sermon about God's acceptance of sinners. Here he committed something of a faux pas by comparing sinners to prostitutes, riddled with foul diseases, but still capable of receiving God's healing love if they turned away from their sin.

"And so I'm asking you today, friends, have you given your soul to worldly corruption?" His eyes and beaky nose searching out weakness, his voice softly pleading, the pastor slowly swept the congregation with a long, pointing finger."Have you given your soul to worldly corruption? Are you filled with impurity? Regrets? Guilt? Are you prostitutes in your hearts? Maybe you believe no one will ever accept you?"

His accusing hand and head dropped for a moment at this discouraging prospect. When he raised his head to look at them again, his face was sorrowful, his voice softly resigned. "Folks, in my work in prison ministry, I encountered many actual prostitutes, and you know what? Jesus did not turn them away when they—oh so bravely—offered him their sinful hearts. More than that, many of them found good, loving Christian men who were able to accept their past, and they went on to live upright, decent, Christian lives."

Without warning Pastor Long took two quick strides to the edge of the altar area and surveyed the souls in his care with burning passion in his eyes, tender fatherliness in his tone. "Now my friends," he said, turning his head to take them all in. "If Jesus could find it in his heart to accept those fallen, sinful women and help them build godly homes, do you really think He can't help you?" He turned his head, running his eyes over them as they considered this.

"O friends," he said, his voice like a sigh, "I'm askin' you to be brave like they were today. Trust in the strength and the love of the risen Jesus, friends, and I just know, without a doubt, that He will come into your heart and just fill it with glory." Pastor Long's dark eyes flamed with the intensity of his vision of God's love, but he held out his long arms out tenderly, as if inviting the whole congregation to shelter there.

#

Dad, what's a prostitute?" asked T. J., on the way home. He remembered the woman getting stabbed in the fiery pit in the Judgment Enclosure and thought that perhaps she had been one, but not repentant, like the ones in Pastor Long had talked about.

Hannah Grace covered her mouth with her hand and exploded with spluttering laughter behind it. "Hannah Grace!" said their mother, reprovingly, turning her thin, frowning face toward the backseat.

"Were you one, Mom?" T. J. persisted. He immediately saw he had made things worse, but didn't understand how. The prostitutes had been the heroines of Pastor Long's story, courageously confessing their past and being accepted by God and good husbands.

His mother's face tightened, and she looked as if she would have hit him if he had not been out of her seat-belted reach. "Why you—" she began, but then her face softened, and she turned to her husband, who had pulled the car over. "I think he really doesn't know, Jake."

His father's face joined his mother's, both peering at him from between the headrests. Hannah Grace was looking at him with pitying incredulity. T. J. felt like an insect specimen. "Zat true, son?" his father asked. "You askin' a serious question?"

T. J. squirmed and prayed silently to God to keep his mouth padlocked in the future. "No—I don't know. Forget I said anything," he muttered, not looking at them.

His father took a deep breath. "A prostitute is someone who sells her body for money, son," he said. "Understand?"

T. J. knew that the best way to end the torment was to lie as frankly as possible. He met his dad's eyes and nodded. "Yes sir."

"All right then. Show's over, Hannah Grace."

T. J. did not look at her as the car pulled away from the curb. At least his mom and dad were facing front again. But how could you sell your body—like, to science? For what, exactly? Organs? Was that sinful?

He felt a sharp poke in his side and saw that Hannah Grace was giving him a meaningful look and pointing at something out the window. No, she was writing on the window with her finger. "H—O." "HO"—"HO"?—*Oh.* T. J.'s face reddened with comprehension. Of course Pastor Long couldn't just use a simple word everybody knew. The rest of the way home T. J. kicked moodily but not too hard at his father's seat while Hannah Grace smirked.

#

The Dillinghams, it appeared, were not the only family to have a conversation like this after Pastor Long's sermon. Over the ensuing week a number of notes and calls containing varying degrees of consternation trickled into the FBCJ office. Eventually Pastor Long even inserted an apology in the FBCJ newsletter, *The Good News Bulletin.* He also gave Chase the unenviable task of working the subject of prostitution into his upcoming lessons on purity for the youth classes.

Word got out to the community of course. For example, poor Macy Munroe had to explain to a nearly hysterical Nel Harrison why Tyler had asked Nel's daughter Emma to be a prostitute when they played house together. The Methodists and milder denominations were by and large shocked, but those who belonged to more rigorous sects, especially the men, believed Pastor Long had shown the gritty faith he was made of when he chose such a strong example, and they were quietly proud of his daring.

XXIII LOVE, PURITY, AND THE TIME THAT NEVER WAS

By Easter the azaleas had already faded, and there had been just enough rain to turn the pink buds of leaves luxuriant green. Dormant kudzu came back to vigorous life and continued its inexorable march across the South, while the more insidious honeysuckle put out delicate tendrils and sweet-smelling white and gold blossoms, belying the ropy tenacity of its invasive spread. As spring progressed, FBCJ prepared for its First Annual Purity Ball, while the Methodists, believing they could safely weather this new offensive, celebrated the season with mission trips and weddings.

Katie felt like Cinderella as she listened to Jenna and Hannah Grace talk about what they would wear and what their dads would wear. Hannah Grace already had her purity ring, but Jenna knew her dad was going to present her with one at the ball. Katie was not even sure she could get her dad to *take* her to the ball, much less spend money on a ring.

Jim was indeed not in a receptive mood. Recently, a former student who had gone on to study voice in college had committed suicide in his junior year. The boy had been shy, studious, talented, and of course, gay. It depressed Jim that young men like Bryan killed themselves so often—because this was not the first such story he had heard, not by a long shot. And he felt guilty that he had not given this boy more help.

He tried to talk to Alessandro about it during one of their biweekly trysts at the violinist's tiny, music-strewn apartment in Branchville, near the NWGSU campus. They had just had vigorous sex, and Jim felt his mind was absolutely clear and open. Alessandro lay facing him, a slight smile on his boyish face, idly caressing his chest.

Jim ran his hand down Alessandro's side, enjoying the tapering from shoulders to hips, the firmness of his thighs. The substantiality of flesh was comforting. "I went to a funeral this morning," Jim began.

"Oh?" The younger man's eyes widened in sympathy. "Anyone I know?"

Jim shook his head. "Nah. Just a young tenor I used to teach piano to. Gay—suicide—you know the story."

Alessandro kissed him gently on the lips. "I *was* da story, *caro*."

Jim got up on one large elbow and stared down at him. "You mean you—and you never told me?"

Alessandro nodded, shading his eyes with his long, dark lashes. "Eet was a long time ago. You must not worry."

"How did you—?"

"Pills," Alessandro said, dreamily. "My father found me. What a *cancan*."

"No—I mean, I was going to ask, was there anyone who—helped you through it?"

Alessandro sat up and reached for his cigarettes and lighter on the bedside table. "I would have to say—Signor Tchaikovsky."

"Come again?"

"Yes. After they pumped my stomach, I took my violin and went into the practice room, and when I came out, seex months later, I could play Tchaikovsky concerto pretty well, so I knew there was a reason why I was put on thees earth."

Jim chuckled and reached up to tousle Erik's hair. "Music saved me too, I reckon. I truly believe it's God's way of telling us He loves us. But it seems like not everybody's so lucky. I just keep thinking, could I have said something to help that poor boy?"

Alessandro looked down at Jim, who was still propped on his elbow. Smoke trickled from his nose and mouth. He lowered his lashes against it. "What would you say? 'Ee's not so bad, living a lie'?"

Jim sighed and threw himself flat on his back. "You always know the right thing to say, don't you, Sandro? Family happens to be important in my life. So sue me."

Alessandro patted Jim's chest. "I do understand. I am not jealous. I would even go so far as to say, if you abandoned them, I would not love you, because what kind of a person does that?

"But not everybody can live a life so—complicated. Would you, if you could choose over again? If you were young and free and had never known your family? Of course not. You would live with me, and we would be happy together." Alessandro waved his cigarette around in a carefree way.

"You saying you're not happy?" Jim enquired, getting up on his elbow again. He was thinking of the pills.

Alessandro took another drag and blew the smoke up towards the ceiling. "I know that you like to call me 'boy,' *caro*, but I am all grown up, believe me. Besides, I have Peter—" he smiled at the look of alarm on Jim's face—"Tchaikovsky."

While Alessandro finished his cigarette, Jim looked up at the light fixture, a complex design of suspended silver orbs. Time was ticking, but Jim no longer had to check his watch, after so many meetings. He wanted to ask Alessandro again what he could have said to Bryan, but he knew there was nothing, nothing short of Alessandro's suggestion of going back in time, living a different life, for all the Bryans to see. But for that to have happened there would have had to be another Jim who was out for Jim to see, who in turn would have had *his* Jim, and so on, all the way back to the beginning of the time that never was.

#

Katie started in on him the next morning at breakfast. "Dad, FBCJ is havin' this purity ball?"

"Oh?" Jim said, not looking up from his paper, but knowing what was coming.

"I was wantin' to know if I could go."

"Of course you can," Jim said, turning over a page. "If we don't have anything else going on—but you'll have to consult your mother about that." Judy was a nurse, and her shift at the hospital wasn't over yet.

"OK, but see, it's like, the dads take the girls."

Jim shut the paper and looked at her. He was still disconcerted by the way makeup changed her face, making her eyes more prominent, her round cheeks more contoured and womanly. "Sorry," he said shortly, and sipped his coffee.

"But Dad, this is really important to me. My friends are goin', and everything."

"Sorry to disappoint them, but *not* going is important to me. In fact, going's against my religion."

"Since when do Methodists not believe in purity?"

Jim pretended to reflect. "Lemme think now. I be*lieve* it dates back to when that fellow Jesus said 'Let he who is without sin cast the first stone.' It's not that we don't believe in purity; it's just we believe love is more important."

Katie finished her egg and clattered her fork into the plate in exasperation. "But they're not *say*ing purity's *more* important."

"They're not?" Jim cut in. "Have they got a love ball?"

She carried her plate and orange juice glass over to the dishwasher and clattered them down on the counter. "You're just determined to be difficult about this, aren't you Dad?"

"Yup," he said, attacking another section of the paper. "That's about the size of it."

Katie knew from long experience that her father could be just the stubbornest man in the world about the most ridiculous things. It would be no use appealing to her mother. Even if she personally were a fan of purity balls, she would never try to make her husband go against his convictions. Katie racked her brains, but she had no big brother, and her uncles and cousins lived too far away. There was only one other option she could think of.

XXIV PURITY LESSONS

All the girls, ages eleven through eighteen, were gathered in the little children's chapel with the little altar and the stained-glass window with the sleeping lamb. The boys were downstairs in the big fellowship hall because Associate Pastor Randle and Mike Hardacre would be teaching them a stick dance for their Warriors for Purity curriculum, but the girls were crowded together. There was a buzz of anticipation and a vaguely festive atmosphere.

Chase Moore sat next to Jenna Whitfield in a front pew to one side, acutely aware of being the only masculine presence in the overflowing room. A few more girls sat down in their pew, and Chase was unavoidably pushed up against Jenna's soft body. She was not his type—in ten years she would be plump, he thought, in twenty as fat as her mother—but sometimes he was perversely fascinated by that prospect. He could imagine her flesh, freed from her dainty white dress, jiggling voluptuously, giving under his touch like deliquescent fruit. Virginal she might be, technically. Pure, he felt sure, she was not.

Around eleven fifteen, Chase got up and explained that today they were going to talk about purity. He told them that whether they knew it or not, they all had some ideas about what it meant to be pure in their words, their actions, and their hearts—but where did these ideas come from? Were they biblical? Today's materialistic, hypersexualized society, he said, might give them the impression that it was OK to throw away their purity as long as it "felt good," but oftentimes people who chose to "live for the moment" realized the spiritual damage they had done only when it was too late. For example, he reminded them, the prostitutes in Pastor Long's Easter sermon had risked being rejected by the world, though not by Jesus, when they confessed their impure sexual past.

He had them all bow their heads and offered a brief prayer that God would bless their class and help them to lead godly lives, pure in heart, word, and deed. Then he had them take their bibles and look at some verses on purity, such as "Flee from sexual sin! No other sin so clearly affects the body as this one does. For sexual immorality is a sin against your own body" (1 Corinthians 6:18); or "Who can find a virtuous and capable wife? She is more precious than rubies" (Proverbs 31:10). Finally, he said that they were going to consider some representations of purity and talk about them in small groups afterward. He invited Jenna Whitfield to come up and give the first demonstration.

Jenna reached down and pulled two red roses out from under her pew. Full of embarrassed self-importance, she ascended the steps to the altar area. "Go, Jenna!" Hannah Grace cheered from the middle of the room, where she was sitting with Katie Engels.

Jenna smiled self-consciously and tossed her long brown hair back. She put one rose on the altar and turned to face them, holding the other one upright.

"Hi," she began. "Our society often gives us the idea that when it comes to our bodies, 'If it feels good, do it.' TV, music, magazines, books, and—" She couldn't remember the other and looked at Chase, who mouthed "Internet" at her. "Internet," she went on, "all show sex as no big deal and seem to say that 'everybody's doing it.' But is this true? Let's take a look at what might happen to someone who—um—buys into these messages."

Jenna looked at her rose. "Let's imagine this rose represents a young woman, perfectly formed by God—let's call her—'Shelby.'" Jenna looked hard at Shelby Gilstrap, who had arrived late as usual with her sister Jordan and was standing at the back of the chapel, glowering defiantly through a lot of black eyeliner. A subdued tittering ran through the room: tittering at the idea of Shelby Gilstrap as God's perfect rose, subdued at the thought of what the thorny Shelby might do to people who laughed at her.

All of Jubilee knew about "those Gilstrap girls." When their divorced mom had become addicted to meth and their grandmother Ruby had taken them, a few years back, they had been known as "those *poor* Gilstrap girls," but not for long. Jordan, the older one, had gotten a scholarship to Jubilee Christian Academy, where she led the basketball and softball teams to national championships and was a dogged, if not stellar, student. Lacking Jordan's brawn, Shelby haphazardly attended Jubilee's junior high and often hung out at Braxton Park with a tough crowd that included some of the town's most disreputable young men, smoking various substances and scaring small children and their parents. Rumor had it she only allowed Jordan to drag her to church because Ruby paid her to go.

Jenna despised Shelby on general principles and knew that this application of her name would get a laugh. Also, she and Hannah Grace and Katie had recently witnessed Zach Finley pick Shelby up from school on his motorcycle one afternoon. Now it was payback time.

Chase was immediately alarmed at Jenna's unchristian departure from the script. He stood up. "Excuse me, J-Jenna. You sure you got that name right?"

"Oh! My bad," Jenna said smoothly, flashing a bright smile in Shelby's direction. "Let's call it 'Shel-*ley*,' 'kay?

"Anyways, Shel-*ley* was at a party, and she met a guy, let's call him 'Bob,' who gave her a beer. Bob seemed nice, and the beer tasted good, after she got used to it, so she had a few more beers, and at the end of the night, when Bob kissed her, her judgment was im—impaired, and her inhibitions were, like, lowered, and so she ended up having sex with him.

"The next day, though, Shel*ley* had a headache, and what was worse was that her conscience told her what she had done was wrong. Bob didn't pay any attention to her, and she felt embarrassed and ashamed." Jenna plucked a petal off the rose and allowed it to flutter daintily to the carpet

So far, so good, Chase thought. As Jenna continued to catalogue poor Shelley's bad decisions and strip away her petals, however, more and more details deviated from the script. Names were changed, tattoos mentioned. Chase felt panic-stricken. He couldn't keep popping up like a jack-in-the-box, but it was clear from the identical glowers on the Gilstrap girls' faces that nerves had been touched. He realized he should put a stop to Jenna's slander, but that might well mean an unpleasant scene with the Whitfields, and Mr. Whitfield was a deacon now, so Chase just sat in paralyzed horror as Jenna ripped away petal after petal.

Finally, after a particularly wild night during which petals showered down on the carpet, the rose was completely denuded. Whether in accidental enthusiasm or on purpose, Jenna had injured the stem of the flower as well, so that it seemed to droop in shame as she turned and picked up the other rose, still perfect and upstanding.

"Finally, Shel*ley* somehow or other met a wonderful, gorgeous, and godly young man—let's call him—" Jenna hesitated, shooting Chase a brief, sideways glance before deciding he could be safely ignored. "Let's call him Zachariah" ("Isaiah," Chase muttered). "Zachariah was godly and handsome—in fact, Shel*ley* finally realized that he was really what she'd been looking for all along. But was it too late? God could accept Shelby—sorry, Shel-*ley*—just the way she was, once she repented. But could Zach?

"After a little time he did decide that he could accept her past. But poor Shelley! She sure did wish she could offer herself with her purity intact, as God intended! But it was just too late." The Shelley rose drooped disconsolately against the Zach rose.

Chase scrambled hurriedly to his feet before the excited whispers and desultory clapping subsided. "Well thank you, J-Jenna. That was certainly—dramatic. And now we'll have one more illustration of purity, from Jordan Gilstrap."

About to descend from the altar area, Jenna froze, looking to the back of the room, where Jordan, carrying a pottery jug, was shouldering girls aside like a linebacker on her way to the center aisle. One side of Shelby's mouth was curved up in an unpleasant half smile. But there was no help for it. Jenna sat down again and waited.

Jordan was not as poised as Jenna. Jenna had even been runner up in the junior category of Jubilee's Stonypoint Quarry Queen Pageant last year and gotten to ride with the other "Rockettes" and the Quarry Queen in the Christmas parade after the junior winner was disqualified for appearing on a *Girls Gone Wild* type video taken by her boyfriend. Nevertheless, Jordan had a certain presence as she glared out from under her thick dark eyebrows like a reproving prophet.

She went behind the altar and thumped the jug down on it. The other girls spontaneously went quiet, so Chase sat down, feeling it was all out of his hands now. "This here's a jug," said Jordan. No one contradicted her. "It's filled with pure, clear water." Still silence, as Jordan dug in the pocket of her skirt. "Would you like to drink it on a hot day?" Jordan asked, following the script. "Well, wouldja?" she insisted, drawing her brows together impressively.

A subdued assent arose, and Jordan nodded, mollified. Then the hand that had been digging in her skirt pocket held up by one wing an enormous cockroach, the kind that could fly. Screams and shrieks arose everywhere The Wilcox twins actually ran out the double door at the back, but then peeked their heads around it just enough to see what happened.

"Quiet!" Jordan shouted menacingly, as Chase got up to quell them. All were stilled, leaving him with nothing to do but sit down again. "Now. S'pose I was to drop this here roach—let's call it 'Jenna'—into the jug." She did so, to general exclamations of "Eww!" and "Gross!"

"*Stop* her," Jenna hissed at Chase, but he just shrugged noncommittally, feeling paralyzed. Jenna folded her arms angrily and jounced back around to face front.

"*Now* who wants to drink this delicious water?" asked Jordan, thrusting the jug out at them. "Nobody? I didn't think so. See, God could keep this disgusting Jenna roach water down, because God can make anything pure. But here in our world, it's a lot harder to deal with impurity, as you can see."

Jordan paused briefly. "OK, that's about it for me," she declared. "Y'all be sweet now." And with that she returned to the back of the room, clutching her jug. This time she did not have to shoulder anyone aside. They maintained a respectful distance. Shelby high-fived her.

Belatedly, Chase lectured them all about using real people in their examples. He made Jenna apologize to Shelby and say something nice about her ("I think you have very—*interesting*—fashion sense, Shelby"); and he made Jordan apologize and say something nice to Jenna ("I'm sorry I called you a big fat roach, Jenna, and I'm sorry your brother got sent to Iraq. I reckon that's hard"). There wasn't enough time for small group discussions after that, so they just closed with a prayer.

#

As Katie waited for the children's chapel to clear out after the purity lesson so she could ask Pastor Moore to take her to the ball, she had no sense of doubt or desperation, even though he was her last resort. It seemed logical that he should assist her in guiding her great power, which he had awakened or revealed, in a godly direction.

For Chase it was not quite the same. The deepening intensity of his obsession with Katie—no, his love, his passionate love for her—made her solitary presence one torment too many, heaped as it was on top of Jenna's and Jordan's purity lessons. That she was spiritually earnest and had golden hair and could dance like an angel only added confusion to the agony of temptation she awakened.

Accordingly, he was a little testy when she said she needed to talk to him. He looked at his watch. "Uh—I'm a little busy just now, g-getting ready for the ball and so forth."

"Actually, it's about the ball."

"Aren't you coming?" he asked hurriedly.

She explained how her father wouldn't take her and her one uncle lived in Savannah and her other ones and her older cousins were all the way in Jacksonville, Florida, and Mobile, Alabama. "But I really want to go," she said. "I mean, not just to go to a ball, but like you said, it's not just another dance. So I was wondering if—" She paused. His heart leapt in exhilarated fear. "I was just thinking maybe you could take me, since it's so important, and my father's—well, I don't know why, but he just refuses. You don't have to buy me a ring or anything," she added, seeing him hesitate.

So cornered, Chase agreed numbly and found himself agreeing to more as he walked briskly to his office and she finalized the details with womanly efficiency. By the time she had taken her glowing smile and slightly breathless gratitude off to torture the rest of the world, Chase felt prepared to face a firing squad, if only there had been one handy.

It seemed appropriate, then, as he stepped from the back door of the Family Life Wing to the rack between the parking lot and the playground where he kept his bicycle, that he should see the brazen Zach Finley leaning backward on the seat of his motorcycle while he kissed Shelby Gilstrap passionately. Too timid and involved in his own torment to intervene, Chase was nevertheless pierced by the sight, even as he busied himself with his bike lock and did not notice Zach and Shelby's captive audience, Jenna Whitfield, waiting next to the door for her parents to pick her up and drive her out to the farm for Sunday dinner with her cousins, who were visiting from over in

Hardwater, on the other side of Branchville.

How old was Zach again? Chase asked himself, finally opening the lock as Jenna was driven away in her parents' minivan and Shelby and Zach broke apart abruptly, wiping their mouths and grinning. Eighteen or even nineteen, Chase thought, not looking as Jordan joined Zach and her sister and there were high fives and laughs at Jenna's expense all round. He, Chase, was only just twenty-four. Yet Zach could take advantage of the poor, troubled girl and no one said a word, while if anyone so much as saw "Pastor Moore" *look* at Katie wrong, his life would be ruined, and this despite or even because of the fact that they actually felt something for each other.

XXV JORDAN GILSTRAP AND THE LOST EMPIRE

Jordan Gilstrap had met poor Miss Sarah Jo, bless her heart, when the Daughters of the Confederacy brought a reenactment of the Incident at Jubilee Junction to Jubilee Christian Academy to celebrate Confederate Heroes Day, back in January. Since the JUMC Fourth of July Celebration, Miss Sarah Jo had retired from her ancestral role, but she still liked for Lydie to bring her to the reenactments, and she liked to lead little seminars accompanying them for the young people, who seemed to have less and less of an idea about who they were and where they came from with each passing year.

Before meeting Miss Sarah Jo, all Jordan had known about her mother's people was that her grandfather had been a sharecropper and her mother had run away from home and been a stripper and possibly worse until she met Jordan's father. The brief bid for middle-class respectability ushered in by her marriage had quickly degenerated when her hours were cut at the Braxton Mills finishing plant (which had still been winding down operations in the mid-nineties). Her husband's drinking and eccentricities made him an unreliable provider. She took an extra job, and to stay alert and lose weight began to take meth, a habit she was unable to control.

Though generous and doting to a fault to the girls, Ruby spoke of her daughter-in-law seldom after she took them in, and then always alluded to her as "no-account," intimating that she had single-handedly driven their father to the excesses that estranged him from his family. She was also anxious about the sisters' coloring, often urging them not to get *too* brown in the sun.

But Sarah Jo told Jordan she had discovered, through genealogical research, that the girls' mother was a direct descendant of Amelia Bowles, the only Creek participant in the Incident. Amelia was the scout who warned the women the Yankees were coming (for the sake of brevity, she had been cut from the JUMC production, after much discussion). Further, Amelia was descended from William Augustus Bowles, the Maryland Tory who married two Native American chieftains' daughters, turned pirate for England against the Spanish, and tried to establish a Muskogee state.

All this warmed Jordan to poor Miss Sarah Jo. Although those Bowles' who had been left behind after the Trail of Tears removal had come down sadly in the world, Jordan walked a little straighter, even with an easy swagger, through the halls of Jubilee Christian after the elderly woman's visit. Her athletic prowess grew to legendary proportions as she found herself more and more in the zone, no longer desperate to prove she was somebody. She no longer felt, as her mother had, that the carefully groomed ladies of Jubilee, with their pitying smiles and quietly self-righteous husbands, were models to aspire to. They and their country-club set were mere parvenus compared to Jordan's ancient lineage. Their civic activities shrank to ant-like proportions when contrasted with the magnificent kingdom envisioned by her illustrious ancestor.

Jordan also grew closer to Shelby, with whom she naturally shared her new knowledge, for she now viewed her sister not as self-destructively anti-social, but rather as the fiercely independent descendant of a pirate and multiple tribal chiefs. What could be more natural to such a person than piercings, tattoos, opportunistic appropriation, and, in leisure hours, the peaceable passing of a blunt among her crew?

The upshot was that Jordan took to visiting Miss Sarah Jo from time to time, and when Lydie was laid up with her phlebitis and Miss Sarah Jo just had temporary, part-time help, Jordan used to stop by a couple of times a week after school. Poor Miss Sarah Jo was still good with her walker on flat ground, bless her heart, but required her wheelchair for hills and rough terrain, so Jordan wheeled the old lady around the neighborhood and listened to her monologues about Jubilee's colorful past and how the town had declined because people didn't pay enough mind to their own history or have the self-respect to keep up their yards properly anymore.

Miss Sarah Jo's home was on Blossom Street, about halfway between the junior high school and His Word Christian bookstore. The road sloped steeply down as it passed the house, and at the foot of the hill was a crosswalk leading to a small park on the other side. Most days, after her prom planning meeting, Jenna Whitfield would get on her bike, pedal laboriously uphill from the junior high, and then sail gloriously down, coasting past JUMC to arrive at His Word, where she would help her mother until she and her bicycle were driven home to dinner.

It so happened, however, that on Thursday after the purity lesson and before the ball, Jordan, who had observed Jenna's routine since Monday, arranged to be wheeling poor Miss Sarah Jo onto the crosswalk just as Jenna came sailing down. This had required some ingenuity on Jordan's part, and some feigned interest in a very ordinary magnolia that happened to grow in a nearby yard, but just as Miss Sarah Jo was getting testy at Jordan's denseness regarding magnolias, Jordan spied Jenna and deftly wheeled the elderly master gardener directly into the path of the oncoming vehicle.

Now Jordan liked Miss Sarah Jo very much, but she was an athlete and reasoned that in the unlikely event that Jenna failed to stop, her own quick reflexes could avoid collision. Probably the biggest danger was the possible shock to poor Miss Sarah Jo's much blessed heart, but as it happened, Miss Sarah Jo was a shade indignant that Jordan had pulled her away before coming to a proper understanding of magnolias and wasn't even fully aware of the danger until Jenna *had* stopped her bike, sailed gracefully over its handlebars, and, as Jordan jerked poor Miss Sarah Jo to safety, landed face down on the asphalt, fracturing her wrist in an attempt to break her fall.

XXVI PREPARATIONS FOR THE BALL

The Purity Ball was a great event for Jubilee—far more prominent than the Purity Warriors' camp out. Presided over jointly by Pastor Long and Pastor Marcus Thornberry, who had succeeded his father at Mt. Zion Baptist, it was FBCJ's first large-scale attempt to reach out to the African American community, and it successfully united the races in shared concern over the licentious exploitation of young women and the necessity of keeping the genies of female sexuality firmly corked in their frail vessels. Once again, JUMC ignored FBCJ's expanding sphere of influence at its peril.

Although FBCJ, as the larger, wealthier, and more commodious church, was hosting the event, Mt. Zion was a full partner in all preparations. For example, Althea Abbott ran the etiquette classes teaching ladylike behavior for the ball banquet with an iron hand in a white kid glove. Woe betide a young lady of whatever complexion who failed to comport herself as if she were attending one of the more formal ceremonies at Buckingham Palace. Katie was mortally afraid of "Mizz Abbott," Jenna was sullenly defiant, though obedient, and Hannah Grace was twice reduced to tears.

The opening dance to honor the occasion could not be integrated. Only one of the African American girls took ballet, and none of the white girls knew how to do praise dancing. So it was settled that the African American girls who participated in praise dance (including the one who also studied ballet) would present a dance under the direction of Artie Tibbets' niece Lacy, to the song "Never Give Up," while Mercedes Finley would choreograph a ballet for the white girls who studied ballet, to Mercy Me's hit, "Spoken For." There was some talk of live music for this, and for the regular ballroom dancing, but this was unanimously quashed by the FBCJ ministerial staff on the grounds that young male performers (they were thinking of Zach) might, however innocently, stir counterproductive emotions in the young ladies' impressionable bosoms. In the end, two elderly deacons, one from each church, were employed as DJ's.

All the girls and many of the male guardians attended at least two mandatory ballroom dance classes, offered separately by each church, and all purchased or had made "modest, ladylike gowns" in "white or demure pastel colors" with coordinated shoes and "suitable" jewelry. Both Macy Munroe and daughters and Rhonda White of White's Tailoring and Alterations were busy day and night making and adjusting these to each young lady's exacting specifications. Purity rings and corsages for the girls and keys for the male guardians were optional, but strongly encouraged as outward symbols of the protective and affectionate bonds to be established, and on the night of the ball each male guardian was to bring a single white rose for each date. At the end of the evening, each young lady would choose one of these from a silver vase and lay it at the foot of the cross as a symbol of chastity dedicated to its ultimate Guardian.

A photographer was employed to take portraits. Purchase was optional, but again, male guardians were strongly urged to bestow as many memorable tokens of the evening as possible on their mercurial charges. A videographer was also part of the service, for those who wanted a keepsake video, and Chase, with Jeff Randle, made a slide show of each girl out of pictures and quotes donated by each male guardian. The quotes were designed to convey what the men found "uniquely precious" about their dates. Each was accompanied by an appropriate bible verse, and all were included in the video and available for viewing on the churches' websites.

This caused some anxiety for Chase, for although Katie chose her photos herself, he, Chase, had to think up what to say about her. He wanted to say something about how appropriate it was that her last name meant "angels," but that seemed too strong. Finally, he settled on saying that he enjoyed getting to know her in youth group, and he believed that her outward grace was a true manifestation of her spiritual godliness. He closed, shamefully aware of the irony, with Galatians 5:16: "So I say, walk by the Spirit, and you will not gratify the desires of the flesh." While within the bounds of propriety, all this did turn out to be a shade on the flowery side, since most dads just talked about how quickly their daughters had moved from dolls to an interest in boys, though a few talked about the first deer their daughters had shot. Galatians 5:16, however, was a popular choice.

#

At last the big evening arrived. All the eligible girls from both churches attended lest they be thought of as sluts, except Lakeisha Durrell, whose father was in the hospital after a serious accident out at the quarry, the Carter twins, whose mother, when asked, would only shake her head and say, "Oh you know *they* no good," and the Gilstrap girls, who had persuaded Ruby that it was too expensive. Katie was by no means the only girl there without a father, however. Several stepfathers, grandfathers, uncles, and one suspiciously handsome cousin had been pressed into service.

Chase did not pick Katie up because he had to help set up the banquet in the fellowship hall, but in the afternoon he biked over to her house on Church Street, several blocks off the main square, to deliver the wrist corsage he had carefully chosen—a single large gardenia tied with a delicate pink ribbon.

On the way over he tried to pedal away the fantasy of kneeling down and gently tying the corsage on Katie's wrist. He imagined feeling her warm pulse racing under her translucent white skin at his touch, and he could feel how her slight trembling would still with anticipation as he gently pressed his lips against her hand. He put his head down and pedaled faster.

By the time he got to Katie's old house, with its big shady chestnut tree and deep porch, Chase was sweaty and red-faced. He parked his bike on the cement path leading up to the porch steps and went to her door, thinking how like Katie this old-fashioned, unassuming home was, right down to the piano music drifting out over the yard.

It stopped abruptly as he rang the bell. There were heavy, hurried footsteps; then the door opened and there was Jim, Katie's father, whom Chase had not met before, standing in the doorway looking his visitor up and down. "Yes?"

He was bigger—both taller and more powerful looking—than Chase had expected. Chase pushed his glasses up on his sweaty nose and put out a hand. "Hello, Mr. Engels. I'm Reverend M-Moore, the youth minister over at First B-Baptist? How you doing today?"

Jim ignored the inquiry and took the hand without enthusiasm. "If you're looking for Katie, I'm afraid she's not here. I believe she's over at Jenna Whitfield's helping her get ready."

Chase had not heard about the accident yet, so he did not ask after Jenna but just said "Oh. Well, not a p-problem, sir, and I won't keep you but a moment," trying not to sound crestfallen. He struggled to free himself from the straps of the book-bag that held the corsage. It seemed to take an age. He felt he should call Mr. Engels out on why he wasn't taking Katie to the ball himself, but there didn't seem to be a tactful way to ask why he didn't want to protect his daughter's purity.

At last Chase extracted the corsage, still perfect in its plastic box, and handed it over to the man. "I just stopped by to g-give her this—" Chase looked at him for some acknowledgement, perhaps even guilt, but he just kept boring steadily into Chase with his gimlety gray eyes.

"I'll see that she gets it," Jim said, not even glancing down at the waxy glory of the flower, the softness of the ribbon. "Now if you'll excuse me, I have a student." He turned on his heel and closed the door in Chase's face.

#

The ball began at 6 p.m. By six twenty or so, most of the young ladies had entered the hall and exclaimed over everything in the murmuring, indoor voices Althea had drilled into them. There were long tables placed end to end around three sides of the large room and covered with real white tablecloths. On each table were two lighted long white candles with wreaths of pink rosebuds and baby's breath at their base. Couples were seated alphabetically, except for Chase and Katie and Jenna and Deacon Whitfield, who all sat at the ministers' central table. At each place were a place card, a place setting, and a goblet with a pink cloth napkin artfully arranged in it to look like a rose. From the center of the ceiling hung a disco ball.

The girls who were in the opening dance came in their costumes—long white tutus for the ballet dancers and long flowing white dresses draped with gold sequined scarves for the praise dancers. They looked over the preparations, greeted a few friends, and disappeared through a door next to the stage at one end of the room, carrying their ball gowns over their arms. Even without Althea's eagle eyes upon them, all the girls felt shy and subdued amidst such grandeur. Jenna, with her scraped face, swollen nose, and wrist in a cast, felt horribly self-conscious, but she was so soothed by the shower of sympathetic attention she received that she even refrained from animosity in recounting the accident, feeling that now was the time to take the high ground.

Katie collected herself while she got ready to dance backstage. She felt funny about being partnered by Reverend Moore—Jenna and Hannah had certainly had their fun at her expense—but also proud, both because she was with a minister, and because her man was the most like a real date. Chase in his tux certainly looked resplendent for the occasion, but so did all the other men, especially Hannah Grace's father in his dress blue police officer's uniform, retired Colonel Don Henderson, Yolanda's older brother, in his dress greens, with medals from Vietnam, and Batavius Arnold, the handsome cousin, who was in his private's dress greens.

Also attending was the guest speaker for the evening, a friend of the Longs named Patricia Honeywell. A noted author of the "Guardian Angel" Christian romances for teens, she had recently produced *Angelic Purity: Saving Ourselves in a Throwaway Culture*. Mrs. Honeywell used words like "special" and "precious" a lot. Like her great friend Melanie Long, she had a sweet smile most of the time and a habit of placing her hand on her heart when moved, as she often was.

XXVII R-E-S-P-E-C-T

When Mrs. Long, who had been helping out backstage, came back and told her husband that all was ready, the dancers trooped out onto the stage, and Pastor Long went to the microphone in front of it. His very appearance caused many young ladies to quail inwardly and remember instances of impurity, but his soft voice made them feel proud and flattered when he welcomed everyone, thanked them for making the commitment to a pure, Christ-centered lifestyle in today's world of "hookups" where too often young women were exploited. He said how thrilled FBCJ was to host this event and how long it had been in the making, and he thanked a long list of friends for their contributions. Finally, he especially thanked Reverend Thornberry and Mount Zion Baptist for partnering with FBCJ in supporting and respecting the Christian young ladies of the Jubilee community. After a brief prayer asking Jesus to bless their efforts and help the young ladies lead "lives worthy of Your grace," he concluded with, "Ladies, tonight is all about you," and invited Reverend Thornberry to give the opening address.

Reverend Marcus Thornberry was around forty years old and somewhat larger and more imposing than his father had been, with a more forceful preaching style. When Pastor Long invited him, he rose from his place at the head table and made his ceremonious way to the microphone, his black robe and purple stole with gold crosses flowing regally in his wake.

"Good evening," he intoned into the mike. Then, in a rising crescendo, raising both robed arms in the air, he continued, "And welcome to the First Annual Purity Ball of Jubi*lee*!" ("Amen!" rang out from several members of his congregation.)

Pastor Thornberry likewise thanked everyone, including his "distinguished and generous colleague, Pastor Long." Then he launched into a homily to introduce the prayer. He said everybody knew they were there to celebrate and support purity, but did they know the best way to do that? Well, he could tell them, but he thought the Queen of Soul, Aretha Franklin, said it best when she said all she wanted—"the *only* thing"—was "a little respect."

"And she spelled it out for us, if you remember—'R-E-S-P-E-C-T.' Well tonight, ladies and gentlemen, *I'm* gonna spell it out for you, and it goes something like this:

"'R' is for rejoicing, which we're doing tonight, but I'm here to tell you, young ladies, when you respect yourself by living in purity, you tend to *get* respect, and when you got respect, outside and in, my daughters, it's time to re*joice*! So that's the first 'R,' 'cause when you got purity, you got something to rejoice over. The bible says, 'Rejoice in the Lord *always*, and again I say, rejoice!' and so that's the first thing we're doing here tonight is rejoicing over all the young ladies and all their gentlemen guardians who are standing up for purity on this very special occasion.

"Now you may say, 'What is so special about purity that we got to rejoice over it?' And my response to that is right there in the second letter of 'respect,' which is an 'e,' and I want you all to think of that 'e' as standing for 'excellence.' Now the word 'excellence' comes from the Latin '*excellere*,' a verb meaning 'to surpass, to go beyond,' and that is exactly what God asks us to do. Romans chapter twelve verse two says, 'Be not con*formed* to the world, but be *trans*formed by the renewing of your mind, so you may prove'—that is, be a living, breathing *proof* of—'that good, and acceptable, and perfect, will of God.'

"And again, Timothy, chapter four verse twelve, says, 'Let no man despise you for your youth; but be an example of the believers, in word, in conversation, in charity, in faith, in *purity*.' And notice how the bible singles out the youth. God doesn't let you make any excuses. He doesn't say, 'Oh she's young, she don't know no better.' No, young ladies, the bible says, 'Let no man despise you for your youth'; in other words, if you want respect, then *as* young people you are specially *called* to be an example of excellence in the *purity* of your life, and I say again, we re*joice* that you have answered the call and are here tonight.

"But ladies and gentlemen, we all know it's not enough just to *want* to be excellent, to *wish* we could surpass the world and worldly ways, and that's why I believe we should think of the 's' in 'respect' as representing 'sobriety.' Now the bible tells us in First Corinthians chapter six, verses nineteen and twenty, that our bodies are temples, and therefore we must glorify them, which means keeping them pure, and we must also glorify the spirit, not cloud it with strong drink or narcotics. And I'm sure you ladies understand that when we *do* cloud our spirit, when we fail to glorify God, is exactly when we start to make even more bad decisions and slide even further down that steep, slippery slope of sin.

"But did you know that 'so*bri*ety,' if you look it up in the dictionary, doesn't just mean 'not under the influence' of alcohol or drugs'? No, 'so*bri*ety' is also the positive quality of having a *se*rious attitude toward life. A serious attitude toward life, and I'm sure if you think for a minute, you'll realize that everyone you respect, everyone who leads a pure life and tries to glorify God, is *se*riously and *so*berly dedicated. And so I applaud all the young ladies and their gentlemen here tonight for their sobriety, their *se*rious dedication to the glory of God.

"So now that we've laid the foundation by re*joi*cing in God's gifts, by striving for excellence, by maintaining so*bri*ety in our actions and our outlook on life—now we're ready to commit to leading a pure and Godly life. And not just tonight, mind you. Tonight it's easy—no temptations, your dedicated guardians right there with you. But you are pledging yourselves to purity for the rest of your lives, no matter what temptations and struggles the world may have in store for you.

"So as you make your covenants tonight, I want you to remember how that 'p' for purity is right there in the middle of 'respect.' Yes, purity is central to your respect for yourself and to earning respect through the example you set by glorifying God—Hallelujah!"

Pastor Thornberry held up his hand, and his congregants responded variously "Hallelujah!" "Praise the Lord!" and "Amen." After a pause, the minister resumed.

"Now we've seen how you can establish purity on a basis of rejoicing, excellence, and sobriety, but once you've done all that, once you leave here tonight, is your work finished?" (Shaking of heads and murmurings of dissent from the audience.) "Are you just gonna say, 'Well God, I guess I done glorified you enough now?'" (a louder "*No*!" from the African American men).

Pastor Thornberry's hand slashed through the air as he thundered, "*No*! I tell you what you're gonna do: you're goin' to *ed*ucate yourself. And not just in school. Yes, you got to study; your studies are important. The bible says, Ephesians chapter four verse eighteen, 'Do not walk with your understanding darkened,' that is, in ignorance, or you will be 'alienated from the life of God.' But you have to study not only God's works, but also His words. Why? So you can know His ways, and walk the way of the Lord *all* the days of your life—Hallelujah!"

"Hallelujah!" and "Amen!" again rang out in response. By now some of the white men were also muttering responses. Pastor Long even said "Amen" quite audibly, by way of making his guest feel at home.

"But I got good news for you," Pastor Thornberry continued. "Good news, which is that you have the greatest teacher in the world to educate you, and that is Christ Jesus—'c,' the next letter in 'respect.'" Pastor Thornberry paused to let them absorb this. "Yes, Christ, the 'light of the world,' will be a 'lamp unto your feet and a light unto your path,' showing you the straight and narrow way of purity, the way of respect, as you go through life—but *on*ly—

listen carefully here, because this is very important—only if you have a re*la*tionship with Him.

"And so that brings me to my very last point, the last letter of 'respect,' and that is 't,' for 'theology.' Yes, theology—'*theo*,' from the Greek, meaning 'God,' and '*logos*,' from the Greek, meaning 'ground or principle of knowledge.' And in the Gospel of John where it says 'In the beginning was the Word, and the Word was God,' that word, in the original Greek is '*logos*,' so 'theology' is the study of God's Word, which is God Himself.

"And only through that study, that education, that the*o*logy can you have the relationship to Jesus that will guide your steps on the path of purity as you go through life and encounter all the obstacles and thorns and temptations that Satan will put in your way—*Can* I have an 'Amen'?"

"Amen!" rang out. Almost all the white men were at least muttering now, and some of the white girls as well.

In closing, Pastor Thornberry asked each guardian to put his hand out, sending energy toward his partner or partners for the evening, and he asked each young lady to stand and reach her hand and energy up toward heaven. He formally prayed that God would bless the ball and support the guardians and the young ladies on the path of purity, so that each of them might enjoy God's gift of respect while rejoicing in excellence, maintaining sobriety, staying pure in word and deed, educating themselves and others in God's works and His will, and most importantly, continuing to grow in Christ and deepen their relationship to Him through theology.

Almost everyone said "Amen" after this except some of the white girls, who felt a little stunned that Pastor Thornberry had gotten so much out of one little word.

XXVIII PRELIMINARY TREATS

The white dancers now left the stage, and the African American praise dancers lined up excitedly, while Lacy Tibbets came down the steps from the stage to announce that the group had chosen "Never Give Up" to dance to. She explained that this song was written in response to the 9/11 attacks and noted that the artist who performed "Never Give Up," Yolanda Adams, had sung it for President Bush and the First Lady at the White House during the 2002 Salute to Gospel Music, where it moved the president to tears. It was therefore, Lacy said, a fitting expression of the young ladies' dedication to showing the world what America stood for through their own excellence and purity. She closed with a short prayer asking Jesus to bless their efforts in dancing and in upholding an example of purity in a fallen world, and then she sat down at her place as Deacon Parker cued the music.

The girls looked very pretty as they twirled in their white dresses, with the gold scarves pinned to stream out behind their arms like wings. Some of their arching and reaching as they mimed finding strength inside may not have seemed much like "real" dancing to some of the white audience, but no one could say it was wild or improper, and the tagline, "Never give up . . . on you," was inspiring to everyone.

The African American girls came and sat down across from their guardians, and Mercedes Finley came down and said how proud she was of all the young ladies who were dedicating themselves to purity, which truly was, as Reverend Thornberry had said, a way of glorifying God. She said Mercy Me's "Spoken For" was a song about the freedom that came from surrendering your earthly self to God's protection, and her dancers had chosen this not only to represent the spiritual meaning of the vows they would make tonight, but also to acknowledge the role of fathers and other guardians as the earthly protectors of their young women. Mercedes humbly prayed that Jesus would inspire this ballet of thanks, gratitude, and worship, making it a fitting tribute to Him and to all trying to live according to God's will in this corrupt, secular world.

As in the Christmas ballet, the young ladies executed gracefully. At the line, "My heart is spoken for," they reached out expressively to their protectors. When the singer sang, "Take this world from me . . ." quietly for the last time, the dancers kissed their hands in a poignant farewell to the audience, and more than one father discreetly dabbed his eyes.

While the dancers changed into their gowns and came and sat down at their places, lady volunteers from both churches, carefully dressed in black skirts or dress pants and white blouses, set out dry chicken breast in a salty cream sauce, canned green beans, snowy whipped instant mashed potatoes, and fluffy white rolls with packets of margarine. In little bowls on the side were salads of iceberg lettuce, purple cabbage, a single cherry tomato, and two cucumber slices, all doused in an aggressive vinaigrette. Beverages were pitchers of very sweet iced tea, powdery lemonade, and ice water. The young ladies selected politely, their gentlemanly guardians poured with gallantry, and the volunteers refilled alertly throughout the repast, which commenced as soon as everyone was settled and Chase, invited by Pastor Long, had said a quick grace.

When it was over, the ladies cleared with miraculous efficiency and produced dessert, a single diminutive scoop of highly sweetened orange sherbet. As consumption of this delicacy declined to a tepid clinking, Pastor Long again rose to his feet, this time to introduce his and his wife's longtime friend, Mrs. Patricia Honeywell.

He said how fortunate they were that this renowned Christian writer was able to take the time to speak to them, and he explained that when he had mentioned the ball, she had immediately rearranged her schedule to accommodate him because she felt addressing young ladies on this subject was an essential part of her life's work. In the unlikely event that anyone present was not familiar with that work, he reminded them that her Christian romances for teens, the award-winning "Guardian Angels" series, was about to become a show, airing Thursdays at 8 p.m. on CFBN, the Christian Family Broadcast Network, and he told them that Doctor Luke Meddlar himself, of the Christian Family Values Association, had personally endorsed Mrs. Honeywell's latest book on the difficulty of standing up for purity in today's world. He read Doctor Meddlar's endorsement from the back of the book and urged everyone to stop by His Word the next day at two thirty, after church and Sunday dinner, for a reading and book signing by Mrs. Honeywell. Without further ado, he presented her.

Mrs. Honeywell was a well-preserved woman in her late thirties with carefully curled blond hair. She rose with one hand clutching at the neck of her silk blouse and as she made her way to the mike across the room she inclined her girlish head from one side to the other, acknowledging the healthy applause. Taking the mike from its stand and cradling it tenderly, she said, with tears in her eyes and a sweet smile on her face, how moved she was to see so many precious young ladies committed to purity in this day and age and so many special fathers and guardians stepping up and taking responsibility to set and maintain a high standard of morality for their precious families. "And you better watch out," she twinkled, shaking a playful finger around the room at them, "because we're going to hold you to it, aren't we, ladies?"

The girls smiled, and a few shook their own fingers playfully at their guardians.

Finally, Mrs. Honeywell said how moving and special both the dances were and how all the girls in their flowing white costumes looked literally just like precious angels. She paused after she said that and took a deep breath. "That's really what I want to talk to you about today. How many of you believe in angels?" All hands went up with Mrs. Honeywell's. "That's beautiful," she murmured. "And how many believe you have personally seen, heard, or been touched by an angel?"

They looked at their friends. About a quarter of them raised their hands, some hesitatingly and a few only after their friends raised theirs. Pastors Long and Thornberry raised their hands firmly, as did Mrs. Honeywell and the deacons. Somewhat surprisingly, to those who had not heard his stories about Vietnam, Colonel Henderson also raised his hand without hesitation. Torn between the wish to appear devout and the imperative to be honest, Chase chose honesty and kept his hand down. If angels were worth anything at all, he felt bitterly, they would have intervened between him and Katie long before now.

"Beautiful," Mrs. Honeywell said again. "And for those of you who didn't raise your hands, don't despair, because I truly believe that angels are everywhere. They're out there, and in your hour of need—even when you don't *know* you need them—they're going to be there for you." She smiled beneficently. The girls, especially those who had read her books, looked dreamily back at her. The men mustered answering smiles to cover their mutinous discomfort.

"But even if we never feel the presence of the angels around us, did you know that as Christians we are called to help do angelic work here on earth? Yes, because the angels, the *elohim*, are God's *messengers*. And as Christians we are called to spread the *mes*sage of Jesus Christ through sharing the gospel. So what I believe—and I talk about this in my book—is that we are all endowed by God with precious angelic qualities, qualities I'm calling our 'inner angels.'" As she said this, the hand not holding the mike detached itself from Mrs. Honeywell's bosom and moved outward in an expansive gesture, as if her own divine messenger were offering its services to the assembly.

She went on to explain that just as healthy food was essential to maintaining a healthy body, so high-quality Christian music, literature, and other entertainment were essential to strengthening their inner angels. Likewise, just as their bodies needed exercise, so their inner angels must be active in spreading the gospel daily by their words and the example they set. If not, the inner angels would grow weaker, and they would no longer be able to help the young ladies to stay on the higher plane of meaningful Christian work God intended for them.

She explained that this was where their guardians came in. Mrs. Honeywell said she knew each and every man in the room saw the inner angel in the special young woman or women he was charged by God to protect. She challenged them to channel their own inner angels to send them the strength they would need to not only live pure lives themselves, but to also watch over and encourage the precious Christian young ladies in their tender care.

In closing, Mrs. Honeywell said that although there were sure to be many obstacles, snares, and temptations on the straight and narrow path of purity, there was one very simple question the young ladies and their guardians could ask whenever difficulties arose, and that was, "What Would Jesus Do?" She explained that while usually the answer to the question would be simple and clear to any committed Christian, we're all aware that knowing what the right thing to do is and doing it are two very different things. Nevertheless, Mrs. Honeywell truly believed that, fortified with their inner angels, their own personal access to God 24/7, and further protected by their special guardians and *their* inner angels, the young ladies would find the strength and resolve to keep the very special vows they would be making on this very special night.

Mrs. Honeywell sat down to applause, but only Mrs. Long and the soppier girls, who were already fans, admired her as much as they did vigorous Pastor Thornberry.

XXIX DEFERRED GRATIFICATION

Pastor Long thanked Mrs. Honeywell and asked that as volunteers cleared away all the tables, the male guardians would come stand beside their companions for the evening. The ladies whisked away the splendors of the feast, and the elderly deacon DJs, with several of the other men, folded up the tables and carried them off, except for the ministers' table. Then the lady volunteers came back with scrolls tied up with white ribbon, which they handed out to each gentleman guardian. Chase tried to hold his as lightly as possible because his hands were sweaty.

Pastor Long said that they had come to that time in the evening when the daughters would sign their purity pledges and the fathers would sign a pledge to protect their daughters' purity. Pastor Long explained that for the purposes of the pledge, "father" signified the role that each male guardian was taking on, regardless of his literal relationship to his "daughter," who was likewise any young lady who was accepting his protection this evening. He reminded them that the pledges they were making were actually vows, which were just like marriage vows because they were promises to God. Finally, he invited any fathers and daughters who had brought tokens for each other to exchange them before signing the pledge and to wear them in future as an outward reminder of the holy vows they were entering into tonight. He then asked them to bow their heads and close their eyes, and he prayed to God to bring a covering and protector for "all our daughters" and to "Keep us always mindful of the promises we make tonight."

Almost before the amens were over, Chase knelt down by Katie's side. He didn't want to wait to see if other guardians were kneeling but hurried to set an example before he got self-conscious. "Uh—Katie," he said, fumbling in his pocket, "I, um, g-got you this ring."

He looked up as he produced the little velvet box. She flushed with pleasure. "Oh, Pastor Moore, you didn't need to go and do that." She put out her hand, but at the same time looked quickly over at Jenna and Hannah Grace, who were not too busy accepting their own tokens to notice. Hannah Grace, who had already gotten her purity ring on her birthday months ago, was staring openly, and Jenna was casting furtive looks while her father struggled to get down on one knee, but Katie didn't care. She was beginning to suspect their jealousy.

Feeling reckless and figuring he would deal with gossip and fallout later, Chase focused on putting the ring on her finger, but it was too big. "I'm sorry. I r-reckon I got the wrong size," he said.

"That's o. k.," Katie said. "I'll just put it on my chain with my cross pendant. See? But first let me look at it."

It was only a twenty-dollar stainless steel ring engraved with "Love is patient, love is kind. 1 Corinthians 13:4." Chase did not want to give grounds for any talk. But Katie read the inscription and said, "I like that verse. You know? And—hey, I got you something too. I tied it to my corsage."

"You hadn't oughta do that," Chase said, helping her untie the silver key from the filmy pink ribbon. Katie too had exercised restraint in her choice. It was just a simple key like the one Chase used for his bike lock, but it was real silver. With nervous clumsiness, Chase dropped it on the floor and bent to recover it. "You like it?" Katie asked anxiously.

"I do," Chase said solemnly. "I'm sorry I don't exactly have a necklace, but I'll put it in my breast p-pocket, OK?"

"OK," Katie said happily. It was just the discreet way she would have wanted. "Can you fasten me?"

While he stood up, she had taken off her necklace and put the ring on it. Now she stood with her back to him like a diminutive wife, looking over her shoulder expectantly.

"Uh—y-yes. Sure thing," Chase said. He put the scroll down on the ground and fumbled with the mechanism for what seemed an eternity. Her neck was warm, and Chase knew his moist hands must feel clammy against it, but she stood patiently with her head down, one hand holding a few tendrils of her upswept hair away from the clasp.

When the thing was finally closed it was time for everyone to recite their pledges together before signing. Chase gave Katie her scroll contract, and she stood with the other girls and read from it: "I pledge my purity to my father, my future husband, and my Creator. I promise before God to keep myself pure in body and spirit so that I can offer myself as a priceless gift if I should marry."

Chase and the men pledged before God to be pure in their own lives and to set an example of spiritual leadership in their homes. They promised to "cover" their daughters "and be their authority as the guide and leader of their families." Then fathers and daughters went up to the head table and signed, side by side.

When everyone was finished and the photographer had set up to take ball portraits on the stage, near the big wooden cross draped with muslin at the back, Deacon Parker, of Mt. Zion, invited fathers and daughters to take the floor, and the music began. The dancing was decorous and staid, despite the disco ball. Jenna grew bored early on and spent a long time in the restroom trying to cover her scrapes and bruises with more makeup before she had her picture taken with her portly father. For Katie and Chase, however, the evening was magically charged.

Katie had only ever kissed once—a boy at a Methodist retreat the preceding summer. In general, she had no respect for boys her age: she thought they were at best goofy, but usually obnoxious. Now, however, Pastor Moore had taken a special interest in her, had even solemnly pledged—and given her a ring, which he didn't have to do. Of course there was always the possibility that she was wrong, that there was no special connection between them, that he would have done as much for any girl in her predicament, but then there was also the way he was the first to go down on one knee (to actually kneel to her!), his nervous stammerings and fumblings, and the careful way he held her at a safe distance as they danced. No, Katie decided, there was definitely something. She couldn't help looking at him with shining eyes.

Finally it was over. All the girls and guardians danced the last waltz together, and then, as the guardians prayed silently for them, each girl chose a white rose from the silver vase where the gentlemen had deposited them and walked up the steps to lay it at the foot of the big wooden cross on the stage as a symbol of dedicating her purity to Jesus.

Katie got her ballet costume, and Chase carried it for her over one arm while giving her the other. He walked her outside and handed her and her tutu into the minivan when her mom came to pick her up. Then he went back in to help put away the chairs, pick up the roses for use in decorating the sanctuary, and get the disco ball down from the ceiling. He remembered to congratulate Pastors Long and Thornberry and their spouses on a successful evening.

At long last he was free to go. He climbed into his pickup truck, still not allowing himself to feel, to think, to remember, and began to drive home. When he got there, however, he kept right on going, veering off onto a state route that meandered past the quarry turn-off and toward the interstate. About a mile before the exit, in a modest house set back from the road, was the A Plus Spa. The small neon sign in the otherwise dark front window read "open" all night. All the girls were Chinese. There was one very slight, young looking one—but she said she was eighteen—that Chase especially liked. He turned up the gravel side road and into the parking lot, with its high board privacy fence. As he got out he could hear splashing from the hot tub and the girls' high-pitched laughter. Jesus would have to wait.

XXX JUMC ON THE ROPES

The purity ball was hailed in the Religion section of *The Jubilee Sentinel* as an inspiring father-daughter event and a shining statement of interracial unity in the face of disturbing contemporary immorality. The pictures of girls of both races looking up adoringly into their fathers' (or male guardians') eyes as they danced were almost universally deemed "precious" by the female population, and Pastor Long's proposal to open the event to all Jubilee churches in future years was received enthusiastically in many quarters. Patricia Honeywell's book signing was well attended, and for a time her volumes flew out of His Word.

Indeed, though no one was so rude as to come out and say so (or even to acknowledge the existence of the struggle), First Baptist looked to be winning the Jesus Wars. While some might be squeamish regarding the theology of Path to Judgment or even the purity ball, everyone agreed that these were consistent with the wonderful seriousness of purpose exemplified in the Joy of Christmas Program, a seriousness felt to be in keeping with the outlook of a nation desperately embattled in the War on Terror.

JUMC, by contrast, was viewed as high-minded to the point of irrelevancy—a little old-fashioned. No one went so far as to declare Reverend Hollifield out of touch, but there were rumors that retirement might be imminent, and plenty of talk about what "fresh blood" might do.

This hunger for decisive leadership reflected uncertainty regarding the Iraq invasion. The President had landed on the deck of an aircraft carrier and, under a large "Mission Accomplished" banner, declared major combat operations over, but the enemy seemed not to care one whit for his authority. More troops were sent over, including more from Jubilee, and more operations were launched, but no matter how many terrorists we swept up, there were always more out there. As John Whitfield wittily opined over

Sunday dinner, there wasn't a thing wrong with Iraq except it was full of Iraqis. "I got nothin' against 'em," he continued, "only they just don't seem to have any concept of civilization over there." Indeed, their lack of appreciation was baffling, and there could only be one explanation: their diabolical religion.

#

Fred Hollifield was typically low key in staff meetings, and this year's Fourth of July Celebration planning meeting was no exception, but Craig Wright, usually a quiet sort, banged his fist on the table and said, "Darn it, we got to show this town how much God loves this country!" And they agreed that this was just the sort of affirmation around which all could rally in these troubled times, while inwardly hoping it would put JUMC back in the spiritual driver's seat.

Braden was not at all abashed when all eyes turned toward him. Not only did he feel himself supremely equal to the task, it gave him an excuse to avoid visiting his mother in Noble. With Brenda's graduation only a year away, she and her mother and his mother had begun to agitate for him to set a firm date and "make plans" for the wedding. Although he had had years to inure himself to this event, the nearer and more certain it got, the more it filled him with depression.

Jim, too, showed himself ready for battle. He took to dropping in on Braden's office once or twice a week to discuss plans for the concert. Braden didn't really mind—Jim was always easy to look at, and there were things to discuss—but for some time now there had been a lack of candor between them that put the music minister on his guard. Jim didn't touch him tenderly or talk either with exuberant drama or unexpected gentleness anymore when they were alone. Braden didn't know why and wouldn't have cared, except that the burden of pretending to be straight all the time was especially irksome for him now, and it would have been nice to acknowledge, however tacitly, their common bond.

Instead, Jim talked about his family—Lynette looking at colleges, Judy's nursing career, and most of all the trouble with Katie. "I'm telling you—take it from Uncle Jimmy—don't ever have daughters," he said gloomily one day.

Braden refused to think of his future family. "Trouble in paradise?" he asked, trying to lighten the mood.

Jim shook his head slowly from side to side. "Braden, honey, you have no idea. Do you know she asked her mother and I to pick out a date when we could come to her baptism at that church over the way?" He jerked his head bitterly in the general direction of FBCJ.

Braden put his head to one side, nonplussed. "Come on now, Jim. You can't be serious. I thought you were going to tell me she was on drugs, or pregnant at the very least."

Jim leaned forward over the desk as if wilting. "Doggone it, Braden, in her case that religion practically *is* a drug. And the other thing could happen too, if you ask me. Tell me something. You ever encounter that youth minister they got over there? Chase—Moore, that was it."

Braden looked up at the ceiling, tapping his chin with his pen. He recalled a skinny, pasty-faced individual he had encountered at a meeting of the Jubilee Ministerial Association and seen around here and there, often on his bike. "We've met. I don't know him to talk to or anything."

"Well if you ask me, like they say, 'that boy ain't right.' And the worst part is, ever since he took Katie to that purity ball, so called, you'd think he hung the moon the way she talks about him."

"Jim," Braden said, teasingly. "You don't mean to tell me *you* never did anything silly over a teenage crush?"

A story that would have interested Braden was not forthcoming. "Dammit, man, I'm telling you it's more serious than that." Jim did not elaborate, but knit his shaggy brows and lapsed into a brooding silence.

"More serious?" Braden said, after a pause, in a serious tone. "Have you talked to Katie? I mean, asked her whether this—Chase person—has done anything—inappropriate?" Braden thought about Mr. Garrett. Having been sixteen at the time and an enthusiastic participant, though uncomfortable afterwards, Braden knew firsthand how murky these waters could be. Not for the first time he wondered if *he* could become as pathetic as Mr. Garrett in fifteen or twenty years. But no. His life was carefully organized.

Jim's response was uncharacteristically venomous. "There's nothing," he sighed. "Nothing I can pin on him, anyway. It's my understanding he's on a mission trip to Uganda, thank the Lord for small favors." He rose abruptly and shook a monitory finger at Braden. "I'm just sayin', you *got* to pull out all the stops on this one, Braden. I think if Katie sees us knock one outa the park, spiritually speaking, she may think twice about that temple of hate over the way."

He stalked out. Braden was surprised Jim made such distinctions. After all, the Methodists officially decreed homosexuality to be sinful every bit as much as the Southern Baptists; they just didn't make as many public statements about it. But not to worry, Braden thought. He was never one to do things by halves.

XXXI REVEREND HOLLIFIELD ON BULLIES

Summer was upon Jubilee. Rita Hill and Marvin Patterson returned from their honeymoon in the North Georgia Mountains still radiant and giggly. Because of the drought, people watered at prescribed times, but enough so that most of the town turned its customary luxuriant green, the magnolias were in blowsy, fragrant bloom, pink, feathery fans of mimosa spread themselves like the invasive wantons they were, and riotous pink and white crepe myrtle blossoms waved flirtatiously everywhere. Soon everyone would start to pick blueberries to bring to occasions or give all their friends, either as is or deliciously baked in pies, buckles, cakes, and all manner of confections.

The JUMC choir was in a jolly but determined mood, ready to stand up for America in these troubled times. Too many members of the bell choir were on vacation for them to perform, but Braden felt that was just as well, since he wanted to go for big sounds and inspiring lyrics. May Ewing's piercing soprano would be helpful when blended into the choir, and he gave her some business in the Cohan medley to placate her for losing her position as leader of the section. Indeed, the only person who gave any trouble was, unexpectedly, Craig Wright, who campaigned hard for Toby Keith's "Courtesy of the Red, White and Blue" to be included on the program, volunteering to sing it himself. With lyrics promising to "put a boot in your ass," in a show of patriotism, the song gave Braden a frisson of distaste, but, ever the diplomat, he hoped he would not be required to give his opinion, especially as it might be deemed unmanly. Cyrus Buell argued forcefully that it was inappropriate to say, let along sing, the word "ass" in church, and the dispute grew heated before Fred Hollifield, who had been turning his head from one antagonist to the other as if at a tennis match, intervened.

"Gentlemen, gentlemen, *please*!" he said, raising his voice over the discussion and waving both arms up and down to quell the rising tempers on both sides of the conference table. Once he had their attention and all was quiet, he turned his smiling, watery eyes toward Youth Pastor Wright, who was smoldering mutinously, and addressed him with even more than his usual patience.

"Craig, I don't believe I've had the pleasure of hearing this song" (he made a deferential gesture toward the lyrics sheet in front of him), "but I can certainly see that it sends a strong, patriotic message about this great, godly country of ours." Reverend Hollifield clenched one fist to emphasize the strength of his agreement with Pastor Wright.

That holy man looked ready to follow up his advantage, but Reverend Hollifield was already turning away from him with a gentle chuckle. "Cyrus, I'm afraid us old folks have to forgive the fiery spirit of youth burning so strong for God and country."

Cyrus forced a smile, though he was only ten years or so older than Craig and resented being lumped in with his septuagenarian superior.

"But quite apart from the vulgar language—which you so rightly noted, Cyrus," Reverend Hollifield continued, waving one arm vaguely behind him to quash possible interjection from Pastor Wright, "Quite apart from anything else, I think we must look at how prominent 'you,' the enemy, is here, and we must ask ourselves, do we want to give them so much attention in *our* celebration of *our* independence?"

Pastor Wright opened his mouth and shut it at the strength and freshness of Reverend Hollifield's simple question. Cyrus Buell's eyebrows shot up in surprise. He held his lyrics sheet up in front of him, his round eyes growing still rounder as he tried to work out the grounds for this new argument.

Braden was about to gabble his support for Reverend Hollifield, but the kindly old man was already off on another tack. "You know," he said, gazing out the big square window at the Wendy's restaurant across Church Street, "this reminds me of what my mother always said about bullies. I never started a fight, but when I used to come home with a black eye, feeling all sorry or myself and at the same time kinda hangdog for disappointing Mamma by fighting, she would just look at me and sorta sorrowfully shake her head"—Reverend Hollifield shook his own slowly from side to side. "Mamma didn't say much to me; she just used to say, 'Freddy, when are you gonna learn to quit givin' 'em the satisfaction?'"

There was a pause. No one wanted to break in on Reverend Hollifield's remembrance of his mamma, about whom they had all heard a good deal—even Braden, though he had only been there a year. Finally, heaving a deep sigh, the old man resumed, "It's taken most of my life to understand even the tiniest fraction of Mamma's wisdom, but I do believe I have figured out what she was trying to tell me all those years ago, and I know that all three of you smart guys understand it, too. We're dang well not gonna give our enemies any satisfaction at *our* Fourth of July Celebration this year, are we,

Braden?"

Braden smiled and saluted smartly. "No *sir*, General. We are keeping our patriotic message one hundred percent positive, *sir*."

"Glad to hear it," said Reverend Hollifield, and the meeting was adjourned.

XXXII THREE CHEERS FOR THE RED, WHITE, AND BLUE

In the young country of America, and especially in the tradition-loving South, rituals take root quickly, and so by the second annual JUMC Fourth of July Celebration, a pleasantly reassuring sense of continuity was already attached to the occasion in the minds of Jubilee's upstanding citizens. If anything, this celebration was more auspicious than the previous one, for the sun shone brightly, as it did nearly every day that drought-ridden summer, and no tremors or thunderclaps marred the proceedings.

There were fewer African Americans in the audience this year, Braden noted—just Yolanda's family members and a few caretakers like Lydie with elderly whites—but that was to be expected now that the theme of the program was different. Overall, attendance was up on the reputation of last year's performance and the need to assert America's strength in the face of the troublesome infidels. Braden could not help but feel his chest swell with pride under his pleated dress shirt.

"Give 'em hell, maestro," said Jim, slapping Braden on the back as he went out to take his place at the organ.

Braden gave a little kick and said, "Oh, it'll be a 'boot in the ass' all right," and Jim, who had not been present at the meeting but had heard all about it, went off chuckling.

As before there was an overture, this time with a larger, louder orchestra on the strength of a new sponsor, Harrison Homes, run by Nel Harrison's gruff, earnest builder husband. Braden's program began relatively low key, with a grandiose blend of "This Land Is Your Land" and the theme from Brahms's first symphony. Reverends Hollifield and Buell then came on to welcome everyone. Reverend Hollifield explained that, "When our nation is—*as* it is today—*at* war, it is--e*speci*ally important to remember the many blessings God—*has* given us and our—*great* nation, and above all, to remember those who—*fight* so that we may enjoy freedom—and to remember all those who—*fought* before them, and all those who gave—*their* lives for God and country." Reverend Buell led everyone in a prayer in which the men and women of our armed services were specially featured.

The choir processed to the hymn, "God of Our Fathers," with Alessandro Trentini's violin soaring beautifully over the rest of the orchestra and singers in the descant to the last verse. Following this came two sing-along audience numbers, "My Country, 'Tis of Thee" and "America the Beautiful," crowned with the choir exuberantly rendering "Columbia, the Gem of the Ocean." Joy Loomis slightly botched the piccolo solo in the opening, but the violins made it through the runs in the first bridge OK, and the orchestra came down well for the men's verse. By the time the choir began the final chorus's "Three cheers for the red, white and blue!" waving little American flags, the audience were all spontaneously clapping to the beat, and Braden turned around on the podium to join them, clapping high over his head. When the song ended, he bravely shouted, "Hip, hip—" over the applause and cheering, and everyone shouted an answering "Hooray!"—all of which was repeated twice for a resounding three cheers, complemented by a stray "Yeehaw!" or two afterwards from some of the younger men.

Next came a salute to George M. Cohan, a lively, lighthearted series of numbers that involved much tossing of sequined top hats. Braden was so pleased that everyone caught the correct top hat at the correct time that he had to dab a tear out of his eyes while conducting, which endeared him to the choir and brought out their best.

In the final number of the medley, "I'm a Yankee Doodle Dandy," May Ewing's ordinarily lanky frame was stupendous when she marched out and sang the final chorus dressed as Uncle Sam, the coffee cans attached to her shoes and covered with red and white striped bell-bottoms giving her a cartoonish height. The whiskers did not look in the least unnatural, and all in all she brought it off with surprising good humor, to everyone's delight.

After the cheering and laughter had died down, Braden announced intermission and went into the choir room to give a brief pep talk. "Choir! Listen up, please, everybody. I just want to say, fan*tas*tic job. Just please keep your focus and remember, you gotta play all four quarters if ya wanna win the game." ("Go-o-o Bears!" yelled out Bob Ragsdale from the back of the room.) "But really, great job. Just keep it up."

"Thank you. Will do, maestro!" said May Ewing, in her stentorian tones, adjusting her sequined vest and hanging up the Uncle Sam costume and whiskers on the costume rack. A hearty chorus of assent and appreciation followed. Braden went back out to the hall, where Brenda and his mother awaited, shining-eyed.

#

The second half began with the same orchestral arrangement of "Johnny Comes Marching Home" Braden had used last year. Then, at Reverend Hollifield's suggestion, Braden, now an established personage in the community, introduced his mother and Brenda, who stood and waved at the crowd like queens.

As they sat down amid murmured commentary from the curious multitude, Braden took up the microphone with a serious expression and announced that they were going to switch gears. Like every nation, ours had endured dark moments and troubled times. Therefore, he explained, this next section of the program would explore the recent terrorist attacks on the World Trade Center and on the Pentagon, but also illustrate the resilience through God that has always carried our nation on from strength to strength through all adversity.

He introduced the first number of this section, Te Deum *for America*, by talking about how up-and-coming Hollywood composer Stuart Hackens had written his now classic Te Deum *for America* for the 2002 Day of Mourning at Ground Zero. Braden explained that "Te Deum" came from "*Te Deum laudamus*," which was Latin for "O God, we praise thee," and that Hackens intended his work not only as a hymn of praise in the face of worldly evil, but also as a call to stand up for all that was best and brightest about our nation, a call that America, with God's help, had always answered.

This number was challenging. The choir buried their heads in their folders during the Latin lyrics and barely made their entrances, and in the orchestra the French horns were a little out of tune and the strings got lost briefly. But on the whole it was noisy and rousing, and the audience felt energized and uplifted by this high cultural touch.

As the screen came down, Braden reminded them that local hero, Mike Abbott, whose mother Althea and older brother Johnny had honored them with their attendance here today, would be honored in the photo montage that accompanied the next song, Alan Jackson's "Where Were You When the World Stopped Turning?"

While they were taking this in, the audience was distracted by Ron Wylie, who strolled onstage, guitar slung over his shoulder, with such an uncharacteristically solemn expression that no one even yelled, "Go for it, Ronny!" or other encouragement. Judy Engels hurriedly placed a stool, and Ron sat down on it, hitching up his guitar and looking out into the middle distance while the small ensemble of instrumentalists got ready to accompany him.

Ron was known to almost everyone in Jubilee as a womanizing romantic daredevil who doted on his dogs and could fix anything with his hands but was innocent of deep thought. He was a perfect fit for a song whose narrator proclaimed his inability to tell "the difference in Iraq and Iran" despite a personal acquaintance with Jesus and God. The audience, most of whom were at least hazy on the whole Iraq/Iran deal, already loved the song; now they loved the singer, too. The women wanted him, the men wanted to be him. Combined with Braden and Reverend Hollifield's carefully selected slideshow, which included pictures of Mike Abbott, among other first responders, the number moved almost everyone to tears at how much they had felt on the occasion and how New York City, previously a faraway place, full of "different" people, had suddenly become their own.

There was a respectful silence after the final chord, broken by a thunderous standing ovation as Roy let his hand fall to his side and jumped up with an incongruous but endearing grin. He bowed rapidly a few times but refrained from any unseemly antics, leaving the stage expeditiously while Judy removed the stool and the screen rolled itself up.

Next the youth choir took the stage, and beside them Lynette, dressed as the Statue of Liberty, one raised arm holding the torch. Above swelling chords from strings and woodwinds, she began the spoken prelude to "Liberty's Song":

"Give me your tired, your poor
Your huddled masses yearning to breathe free,
The wretched refuse of your teeming shore;
Send these, the homeless, tempest-tost to me,
I lift my lamp beside the golden door!"

The audience started as the voice of Marvin Patterson, invisible at the back of the choir, boomed out in response:

"'The meek shall inherit the earth,' I said,
And so I raised up a great nation,
Rocked in the cradle of liberty,
Swaddled in justice, nursed on hope."

Lynette continued:

"Today in pain, beleaguered and attacked,
I stand as I have always stood,
For this one nation, under God,
Indivisible,
With liberty and justice for all."

As she spoke of pain, the Youth Choir began a haunted oo-ing and aahing that continued through Marvin-Jesus' answering speech:

"I stand beside my people,
Stretching forth almighty power in a blessing:
May you rise up against our common foes!
So may your torch again burn clear and bright,
Welcoming the masses to this hallowed shore."

Now the oos and aahs were in close, keening harmony. The audience felt stretched to the breaking point with fervor as the youth choir, their weak voices barely audible even above muted strings, began to sing "Give me your tired . . . " in an almost spooky setting. The triumphant, hymn-like last two lines about the "tempest-tost" and the "golden door" were a welcome release, even though the sopranos didn't quite hit their last high note in "tempest-tost to *me*."

There was healthy applause, which the kids acknowledged with self-conscious gravity, and Braden invited everyone to stand and say the Pledge of Allegiance. All did so solemnly, many still emphasizing the "under God" phrase that the liberals had attacked.

The choir then sang, "This Is My Country," proudly proclaiming their allegiance to "*my* country! Grandest on earth!" This was followed by a full-scale choral and orchestral arrangement of Lee Greenwood's "God bless the U. S. A." The men, who sang the introductory verse, sounded stronger than usual as they proclaimed that "they" couldn't "take away" the "freedom" symbolized by the flag. In the last repetition of the chorus, "I'm proud to be an American," the glorious string accompaniment was perfectly in tune, and even though the sopranos, "oo-ing" like backup singers, were not quite on pitch, a couple of audience members couldn't help joining in, and everyone sat up a little straighter at the thought of standing up to defend our blessed country. At the end there was cheering and a standing ovation.

Beaming, Braden introduced the offering, which he kept the same as last year—the stirring pairing of "Onward Christian Soldiers" with Mouret's Rondeau, a piece familiar to many from PBS's *Masterpiece Theater.* Braden reminded the audience that magnificent concerts of this caliber didn't come cheap, and was gratified to see the offering plates heaped full.

Following this was the "Salute to the Armed Forces," again preceded by the posting of the colors and the invitation to all who served and their families to stand and be honored. This time, however, Braden prefaced the salute by explaining how important it was to support our troops when we were, as now, in a time of war. After the salute he explained that the last section of the program would celebrate the determination of America's military. First would come the lighthearted "Over There," which had sent American troops overseas to win World War I. Then the solemn "Battle Hymn of the Republic" would, Braden explained (still carefully, for the benefit of

Confederate holdouts), proclaim the Christian roots of our country's strength. Irving Berlin's classic "God Bless America" would express our prayerful hope that God would continue to bless our great nation. Braden noted how privileged they were to have Yolanda Tibbets back again this year to sing the solo on these last two numbers, and there was a ripple of applause. Finally, he announced, "The Star-Spangled Banner" would conclude the concert. He did not announce the confetti cannon, but the audience was not deprived of this now anticipated treat.

#

After this uplifting, universally acclaimed event, the Jesus Wars appeared to have reached a stalemate. While a hardcore minority continued to feel that JUMC was a spiritual lightweight, especially when it came to moral discipline and clean living, there was no denying the timely relevance of their patriotic message this Fourth of July. Talk of Reverend Hollifield's imminent retirement died down, and many among his congregation felt that by directly engaging the War on Terror, their church had more intensely involved itself in the great spiritual battle of our time, for what was that war but a clear-cut struggle of good versus evil?

Most of the good people of Jubilee, however, took a middle ground and, whatever faith they professed, rejoiced in the rich array of spiritual and cultural experiences offered by *both* venerable houses of God.

XXXIII BAPTISM AND BACKSLIDING

It was fall, and football was in every worthy heart. Katie was baptized, but felt herself overshadowed by a delegation of the Fellowship of Christian Athletes that was vising from NWGSU. Katie felt there was no way her baptism could compete with that of nine cheerleaders, a second-string quarterback, two defensive linemen, and the assistant offensive coordinator. Still, she believed Pastor Moore was proud of her, and both her parents attended, though her father would hardly say a word about it, and her mother just sighed and said she supposed Katie was growing up and had to make her own decisions, though no one in the family that *she* knew of had ever been a Baptist.

Katie was not wrong about Chase. On his return from Uganda he had found her lovelier and more tormenting than ever. She often gazed at him at youth group meetings and fingered her purity ring, which always hung round her neck, as if to remind him of their special connection, and she always lit up with a kind, happy smile whenever she happened to see him.

As before, Chase tried to distract himself by every conceivable method, but he was by himself too often. He could not stop himself, sleeping and waking, from building up elaborate fantasies in which he tricked or convinced her into performing the nastiest acts he and his internet purveyors could imagine, while she nevertheless maintained a Christian sense of gratitude, obligation, wanting to please, that left her sweet vulnerability intact.

#

One fine October Monday, Jenna, Katie, and Hannah Grace were sitting in their new, lowlier lunch territory, a little to one side of where the popular older girls lunched (those not eating with boyfriends), on a slope behind the high school.

Jenna began it. "So Katie, who are you going to Homecoming with? Pervy P-Pastor M-Moore?"

Hannah Grace started to give a surprised laugh and had to cover her mouth so her partially chewed chicken finger wouldn't burst out.

"Cut it out, Jenna," Katie said, annoyed. Pastor Moore would never be interested in any of their stupid high-school dances. She would have to decide which of the two sophomores likely to ask her could be trusted to keep his hands to himself. "If you really want to know, I haven't decided yet."

"You're so lucky, being in the Court," Hannah Grace said to Jenna.

Jenna gave a pleased smile. "I know, right? Remember how hard we worked on those posters? I couldn't have done it without my besties." She spread her arms wide, and her protégées leaned in for an awkward hug.

"But to be honest with you," Jenna continued, "sometimes I just think this whole thing —" she swept her arm expansively to take in the high school, the parking lot, and even the most popular clump of senior girls—"is just so juvenile."

Katie was startled to hear her own private opinion from the lips of Jenna, who had been anticipating high school since at least second grade.

"Yeah," said Hannah Grace, assuming a worldly-wise expression and taking out her lip-gloss for a refresher coat. "I know what you mean."

"Should we tell her?" Jenna asked gleefully.

"If *you* think she can handle it," said Hannah Grace, indifferently.

"What?" said Katie, annoyed again.

"Well," Jenna began, portentously, "My cousin, Will, he's in a fraternity over at NWGSU—Omega Phi?"

"Yes?" said Katie, warily. She thought she knew where this was headed now and wasn't sure how she felt about it, even though she was also mad that they had talked it over between themselves before telling her.

"Well, he brought a friend of his, one of the brothers, to our family dinner yesterday, and this guy—I think his name's Taylor? Anyways, I was hanging out with them, and then later Will told me Taylor kinda likes me—whatever. But so, the deal is, they're havin' a big party, and they said they might could get me and a couple of friends in."

Katie looked from Jenna to Hannah Grace and back, feeling shocked. Did the vows they'd made to God not mean *any*thing to them? But if she called them on it, they'd just tease her about being "in love" with "pervy Pastor Moore." "I don't know," she said doubtfully.

Hannah Grace rolled her eyes. "I told you she'd be like this," she said to Jenna.

"But wait," Jenna went on, a note of pleading in her voice. "You haven't even heard the best part, Katie. Clear Blue Sky is doing the music!"

This was temptation indeed. Clear Blue Sky was Zach's band. "But my parents—" Katie began, weakening.

"'My *pa*rents!'" Hannah Grace exclaimed, in high-pitched mock panic. "'And Pastor Moore! What would *he* say?'"

"He'd be jealous," said Jenna. "Probly stalk us to the party. Come on, Katie, are you gonna come with or just sit around with your phone, waiting for 'P-Pastor M-Moore' to call?"

"'Hello K-Katie,'" said Hannah Grace, holding an imaginary phone to her ear and imitating her uncle's nervous, serious manner. "'I have s-something to s-s-say to you—" and Hannah Grace panted heavily into her imaginary phone like a dirty caller.

"Quit already," said Katie, throwing a tuft of grass at her. "You guys wear me out, I swear. I just gotta think of what to tell my parents."

XXXIV GOOD AND BAD APPLES

Very early on a Sunday morning a few weeks later, Chase was disconsolately wheeling his bike along State Route 390, aka Branch Road, which ran between Branchville and Jubilee. He had gone for a long ride out on little-used dirt roads, whirring past sheds with signs reading "Antiques" or "Madame Sophia, Palm Reader and Psychic," past trailers in varying states of repair, past cinderblock buildings with no windows where single moms stripped for tired farmers and quarry workers, through farming communities, with their humble churches, and even into rows and rows of the cheapest quick-growing pine, for out beyond the quarry it was all timber country in that direction, until you got to Johnson Lake.

Returning, Chase had a close call with a weaving, rusty pickup, and in swerving hit a rock, causing a flat tire and some damage to the wheel as well. He'd have to have a look later, but he could tell a mere roadside repair wouldn't do the trick. And so, though his legs felt rubbery and strange, he was forced to dismount and wheel the thing home. He headed for Branch Road because it was better lit and patrolled, and therefore less likely to have crazy drunks careening around on it at two of a Sunday morning.

At first his mind was clear and light, and as he worked his fatigued legs, he dreamed his dream of one day heading up a renowned summer camp for Christian youth, where every night they would all sit around the fire, singing praise songs with the love of Jesus in their hearts. He thought of the songs they would sing, the regular bumping of the bent wheel rolling over the gravel keeping time to the music in his head. He pictured the firelight gleaming on the young faces, their hair, their legs, those wonderfully smooth, inviting legs the girls had. . . . As usual, Satan had gotten into the details somewhere, and Katie was never far behind.

It seemed fitting that just as he grasped her silky thigh in imagination, a fork of lightning split the clouds, closely followed by a resounding thunderclap and a sudden downpour, the first real wetting in months. Chase was quickly soaked through, in spite of his helmet, but he kept trudging doggedly onward. Everything was closed at that time of night, but if he could just make it up to the Quik Stop ahead, he could rest up under the eves of the minimart and even sit down for a while.

As he neared the darkened building, however, he was surprised to see a smallish car towing a trailer turn into the pumping area. It circled around until it was pointing back at the road again, with the driver's side nearest Chase. The window rolled down, and Chase heard himself being hailed.

"Yo! Pastor Moore! I *thought* that was you. What in the world are you doing out here at this time of night?"

Zach Finley was far from Chase's favorite person, not least because, although he was barely out of high school, he never even considered addressing Chase as "sir." Still, at that moment Chase felt he had never been so glad to see anyone in his life. "Hey, thanks, buddy," he said, approaching the car.

Zach had already rolled up the window and was out and opening the trailer doors. "Lemme see," he said, peering into the mess of speakers, drum kit, and guitars. "It's pretty crowded, but if we take your front wheel off, I reckon we can fit your bike in here."

"OK. I'll get the brake," Chase said, fumbling at the cable.

"I got it—here. My hands are dryer'n yours," Zach said, releasing first the brake and then the wheel speedily and (Chase thought) officiously. "Looks like you had an encounter with a rock," Zach added, as he noticed the damage. Irritated though he was over being caught at such a disadvantage by this Lothario, Chase was grateful to climb into his Dodge Neon.

"Hoo, boy," Zach sighed, settling into the driver's seat and slamming his door. "Bet you're glad to be outa that rain. I know I am, and I only got a few minutes of it."

Chase ignored this. He felt Zach was rubbing his nose in his own need and the youth's beneficence. Besides, he seemed to be sitting on something. He held it up awkwardly and an object fell out onto the floor.

"Oh, sorry about my jacket," Zach was saying, as Chase bent down to pick up the item. Holding it up to the light coming through from the street, he could see it was a plastic zip-lock baggy full of round, white pills. Chase continued to hold it up, looking questioningly at Zach, trying not to let his triumph show.

Zach was not as perturbed as he should have been. "I'm not gonna lie to you, Pastor. They're roofies. Maybe you can advise me what to do with 'em."

Roofies? Date rape drugs? This was more dastardly than even Chase could have imagined. He opened and closed his mouth a few times, but couldn't frame words.

Zach continued insouciant. "Now don't look at me like *that*. They ain't *mine.*"

"Oh?" Chase said. Hoping Zach would reveal unexpected depths of depravity, he tried to sound nonjudgmental.

But Zach was unruffled. "No, I got 'em offa some fool college boy at the Omega Phi party we was playin'"

"You did?" Chase asked, still trying to sound open. He put the baggy on the seat beside him and tried futilely to warm himself with his arms. He wished he could take off his soaked shirt, but it seemed more polite to wait till he was home.

Zach started the car and pulled carefully onto Branch Road, the ponderous trailer swinging out after them. "I don't know if I done the right thing or not, Pastor," he said, reflectively. "*You're* the expert on that, I reckon."

"What did you d-do?" Chase asked. Now it would all come out, he thought grimly.

"Well, first of all, I see these underage girls I know from church come into the party we was playin' tonight."

"Who?" Chase said eagerly.

Zach flicked his eyes in Chase's direction, then back to the road. "I don't wanna get anyone into trouble. Off the record?"

"Of course."

"All right. The Whitfield girl, the Dillingham girl—Hannah? And that other one, hangs out with them."

"K-Katie," Chase managed, looking straight ahead, rigid with apprehension.

"Right. Well, those are the ones I recognized, anyway. No telling how many there were, of course. Underage, I mean. You been to college. You know how these things go."

Chase nodded. He knew exactly.

"Well, then I seen this jackass slip one of these into the Whitfield girl's drink. He didn't think anyone would notice, but the band was kind of up on a stage, you know, so I saw the whole thing."

Chase nodded and swallowed, his mind racing with possibilities, the most pleasurable of which involved Hannah Grace's daddy throwing the whole lot of them in jail—Zach included.

"Well, I don't know as you would agree with how I handled it an' all," Zach said cautiously. "I coulda called the police, but I calculated by the time they came, it might be too late for that Whitfield girl." Zach sighed, moving into a confessional mode. "And I gotta admit, I know which side my bread's buttered on. We make a lotta money off fraternity and sorority gigs. I didn't see a point in burnin' down the orchard on account of one bad apple, if you get my drift."

Chase nodded again.

"But I didn't just sit on my hands either," Zach hastened to add. "I called a break and took the guy aside for a chat."

"A ch-chat?"

"Yeah. You know, I explained to him about how the university might turn a blind eye to his shenanigans with a college-age young lady, but it'd be quite another matter with a high school girl, an' I pointed out Hannah Grace an' filled the guy in on her daddy bein' a police officer an' all. I was pretty persuasive." Zach gave a grin that seemed unnecessarily smug to Chase.

"And he just *g-gave* you the whole bag?" Chase asked, still suppressing any hint of ironic incredulity.

"Put it this way," Zach said, with another grin. "He could tell I knew how to handle myself. I reckon he figured he didn't have much choice in the matter."

"But you d-didn't get rid of them?" Chase asked.

"To be honest, I clean forgot," Zach said. "The energy was unbelievable out there tonight. I got so caught up in it, I didn't think about those things until they fell outa my pocket just now."

"Maybe I better t-take charge of them," Chase said, watching Zach carefully.

"Please," Zach said, waving his hand as though to keep the pills away. "They're nothin' but trouble. I'm lucky I didn't get pulled over."

Reluctantly, Chase decided to believe him. But he wasn't getting off scot-free. "I think you did the best you c-could, Zach," he stammered, trying to sound pastoral. "But another t-time you really should inform the authorities. This is a serious m-matter."

"You bet, Pastor," Zach said, as he pulled carefully into the parking lot of Chase's apartment building.

#

Chase decided not to tell on the girls or the fraternity. Zach had asked for confidentiality, and not only his employment prospects but even possibly his liberty could be at risk were a full-scale scandal to erupt. Furthermore, the fraternity, the university, and more importantly the girls and their families would be shamed and publicly hurt, all for the actions of, most probably, one bad apple, as Zach had put it. Whatever was done, Chase thought, Katie must not be hurt.

Chase was the more loath to embroil the fraternity in any investigation because he himself was a member, having been active just a few years previously. But he did arrange a private talk with its president, who at least professed shock and promised to take measures. Even if he were complicit, Chase thought, this would let him know that Omega Phi had had a narrow escape and might not be so lucky next time.

Chase also set aside a portion of his youth class for girls and their purity guardians to attend, and in it he discussed parties and the dangers they posed to purity in as frank terms as he dared, and he put up pictures of roofies, explaining how they were used.

Katie was alarmed, as Chase had intended, but Jenna and Hannah Grace merely vowed to be vigilant on their own and each other's behalf from here on out. Jenna even joked to Katie and Hannah Grace that Zach must have spilled her drink at the party on purpose because Taylor roofied it.

Chase thought his precautions were sufficient for the regular girls, but for Katie he was determined to go the extra mile. That was perhaps why, late on many weekend nights that fall, he could be found in the big magnolia behind Katie's house with a pair of binoculars, peering through the leaves into the windows. If Katie was there, he generally watched until she went to bed; if she wasn't, he walked quietly around to the front and up the block to his truck, where he waited until someone (usually Mrs. Whitfield or Mrs. Dillingham) dropped her off, or, if she was sleeping over somewhere, until midnight, when he would drive home, tense and exhausted.

XXXV EARTH-SHAKING REVELATIONS

After the rain in October a few sinkholes opened, but there was no major property damage until November, when the tremors began again. Delia Rosenbaum, who for some time had been noticeable only as one of the growing number of women in black protesting the wars on the corner of the square every Thursday afternoon, again became a prominent figure about town. Besides assessing risk for property owners and their insurers, she also alerted the community, through letters to the *Jubilee Sentinel* and communications to the city fathers, that the NWGSU archeological site known as the Indian Village, some five miles southeast of town, was at risk, While the fate of this historic treasure lies, strictly speaking, outside the confines of this narrative (I believe it was at least partially salvaged), those interested in Jordan Gilstrap may like to know that she began volunteering at the site upon reading one of Delia's letters, and that their relationship, at first academic but in the fullness of time romantic, began there.

But to return, the tremors and more rain multiplied the sinkholes, and there was cultural and personal loss as well, when Alessandro Trentini, on his way to a gig with the Macon Symphony, swerved to avoid a deer and was struck by an oncoming truck and killed.

#

About a week later, Judy Engels was working the night shift at the hospital, Lynette was away checking out colleges, and Katie was over at Hannah Grace's listening to her griping about how Jenna didn't have time for any of her friends now that she was seeing a college boy and speculating about whether Jenna gave him head. Jim was sitting, as he often did lately, alone at the dining room table, staring into the room's reflection in the front window and wondering at his ability to go on mechanically doing things day after meaningless day, when the doorbell rang.

It was Braden. "Surprise!" he said, making jazz hands, and then as Jim just stood there looking at him, he started to gabble. "You were sick last Sunday, and then I didn't see you around, and you weren't at Sandro's memorial service, so I just thought I'd, you know, drop by and see how you . . ." Braden trailed off. Jim had winced when he mentioned Alessandro, and now two tears were making their way from the outer corners of his gray eyes down through the network of tiny lines around them.

Braden stepped inside as Jim mutely gave way. "Oh my God," Braden said, in a low voice, laying his hand on Jim's arm. "He told me he was seeing someone. It was *you*? All this time?"

Still unable to speak, Jim nodded twice, and then threw his arms around Braden's neck and collapsed sobbing against him. Braden patted him helplessly, keeping an eye out over Jim's shoulder for intruders.

When Jim had subsided a little, Braden said into the ear nearest his mouth, "Jim, Jim honey—is anybody else home?" and was relieved to see the big shaggy head shake "No."

"OK. That's good. That's good, Jim." Gently Braden pushed the big man off of him, though he still held his arms. "Jim I can't leave you like this," he said, looking into the numb, blank face. "Let your Auntie Braden make you a cup of tea. We're gonna take this to God, OK?"

Jim nodded, and holding Braden's hand led the way to the kitchen, since Braden had never been in his house before. While Braden made tea, Jim sat at the kitchen table and pointed out where things were—tea, kettle, teapot, mugs. It had been raining before, and now it was still pitch dark outside, but whereas the reflection of the dining room had seemed as cold and lonely as the moon, now Jim, looking at the reflection of the kitchen in the glass doors to the deck, felt wrapped in a bright, cozy blanket of light, comfort, and warmth through which Braden and his reflection bustled like a dynamo.

Jim blew his nose on a paper napkin and went to the sink to splash some cold water on his face. "The worst part was not being able to tell anyone how I felt," he said.

Braden nodded, setting the mugs down. He patted Jim's chair. "I know," he said. "But I'm here now. Sit. And tell me anything you want."

Heavily, Jim sat. "I wanted to go to that service over at the university," he began, his voice breaking. "But I just knew I couldn't handle it. The whole *world* would've known."

Braden moved his chair closer to Jim's and rubbed his back through his flannel shirt. "Of course," he said. "Don't beat yourself up about it. You know if he could speak to you now he'd understand."

Jim put his head down on his arms. "Oh Lord. That boy understood me better'n anyone in my whole *life*."

Braden stroked his hair. "You know you'll see him again, don't you?"

Jim picked his head up. "Yes. Yes I do believe that, and it's a comfort, make no mistake. Might come as a bit of a shock to Judy," he added, with a little of his customary twinkle.

Braden pushed his shoulder. "Don't you worry about that. You know Jesus has it all worked out."

They took their tea and sat together on Jim and Judy's big flowery sofa in the living room, which also looked out on the deck. Braden put his arm around Jim and snuggled the big man up against himself. "You wanna pray about it?" he asked.

"Not really," Jim said. "I like to go to Jesus on my own, if you don't mind. But I am grateful to you. Maybe it was keeping it bottled up all that time, but you know, before you stopped by, I didn't even feel like I could pray about it.

Braden played with Jim's hair. "It's funny how things work out," he said dreamily. "I used to think me and you—"

"Did you?" Jim rumbled, sitting up and turning his face toward Braden's.

Without warning, Braden was being kissed. Not just kissed, though very much, deeply, exploringly kissed, but also swept into the circle of Jim's strong arms, pressed up against his broad chest, enfolded in flannel, enveloped in Jim's smell of soap and—they must have had a fire earlier—wood smoke. And the kiss itself, which went on and on, now probing, now pulling back, was like a tantalizing promise that made Braden ache with longing and desire and an unexpected sadness.

When Jim finally pulled away, he looked at Braden like someone waking from a mad dream, and Braden could only look back, lips parted, famished for more but not daring to hope.

Just as Jim drew breath to speak, the earth moved. A wrought-iron cross rattled against the wall. Katie's picture fell off the mantelpiece, and the glass in the frame broke. Outside there was a crash, as of something heavy falling through branches, followed by a thud and a cry. Jim sprang to his feet as if relieved to be galvanized into action. "What in God's name?"

"There's someone *out* there!" Braden said. Fear came over him like a frost, settling on every other feeling with an icy death grip.

Jim charged outside, and after a moment's hesitation, Braden followed. From the deck, he saw Jim bring down a slim figure with a diving tackle that would have made Artie Tibbets proud. Thinking quickly, Braden ducked back inside and turned on the outside lights.

By the time he came back out and down the steps, Jim and Chase Moore were standing up facing each other, breathing heavily. Chase had just been leaving as Braden's car pulled up. At first he had waited to see if Katie were being dropped off; then the intimate, emotional attitudes of the two men had fascinated him, and finally the kiss paralyzed him with horror.

"Don't t-touch me!" he said now, putting his hands out to ward Jim off and looking around for an escape route.

"Don't even think about runnin' off," Jim growled. "You're not going anywhere till you tell me what the hell you were doing up in my magnolia with *these*"—he held up Chase's binoculars.

Chase grabbed at them, but Jim jerked them away. "I don't expect you t-to understand," Chase said boldly. "I've been checking on K-Katie."

"This is unbelievable," Braden broke in. "You're Chase Moore, aren't you? *Pastor* Moore?"

"I see you've been introduced," Jim said grimly. "Now you listen, *Pastor*, and listen good. I don't know what you think you saw tonight, and quite frankly, I don't care. But I'm damned if you come around here sniffing after my daughter. I think you'd best clear off and stay the hell away if you know what's good for you—and that goes for the rest of your holy rolling crew as well!" Jim took a step toward Chase. "Go on. Git," he said. "Before I call the police!"

But Chase stood his ground. "Oh I wouldn't d-do that if I was you," he said.

"The hell you say! Clear off, you little pervert. And don't let me catch you around here again."

"P-pervert!" Chase screamed shrilly, with a maniacal giggle. His many long months—years, really, of frustration and self-denial seemed to blaze up like dry kindling at the word. "You know, I always wondered what k-kind of a man wouldn't look after his own daughter?—No! Let me f-finish," he said, raising a hand as Jim started to lurch toward him again. "Now I know," Chase continued more quietly. "So I'm c-calling the shots, because you d-don't want me telling t-tales out of school now, do you? *Do* you?" he repeated, turning to Braden as well. Neither man spoke.

Nodding, Chase continued. "Now, maybe I didn't go about it in the best way, but I was c-concerned about Katie because I found out—accidentally—that she and her friends lied to their parents and went to a c-college party where date rape drugs were being used." Chase paused to let this have an impact. The fight had gone out of Jim. He was peering at Chase with alert concentration, trying to read his face in the darkness.

"I was able to discreetly c-confiscate the drugs that time," Chase continued, mentally erasing Zach from the picture. "But I c-couldn't help being concerned. As their pastor, I d-do feel responsible for these girls. You of all people should understand, as her f-father." Chase appealed to Jim, who nodded grudgingly. "So I, once in a while, just—ch-checked on them. I just c-can't help myself. That's all. Now you know."

There was silence, broken only by a lonely dog barking a few houses away. Slowly Jim handed Chase the binoculars. "I guess I should thank you for telling me," Jim said. "Better late than never, hey?"

"I'm sorry," Chase said. "I never meant to c-cause all this trouble. And I don't aim to c-cause any more, provided we're all friends?" He put out a hand for Jim to shake.

Jim accepted the hand as briefly as he could.

#

Back in the house, Jim sat heavily on the sofa, and Braden began putting the tea things away in an agitated manner. "This is not good," he said, raising his voice to be heard over the clatter he was making. "Not. Good. I'm telling you."

Jim had put Katie's picture back on the mantel and was gathering up the fragments of glass from the floor. "Aw, keep your hair on," he said, raising his voice likewise. "Even if he does decide to shoot his mouth off, who's gonna believe anything comin' from *that* little rat?"

Braden came and stood in the doorway, drying a mug. "Did you believe him? About Katie? And why he was—peeping?"

Jim shrugged and followed Braden back into the kitchen to throw away the glass fragments. "I believe Katie and me are overdue for a heart to heart. Other than that, I'm not gonna get hot and bothered. Life's too short."

Seeing Jim did not want to discuss the situation further, Braden nodded, and Jim returned to the living room. Braden put the mug and dish towel away and went to sit next to Jim on the sofa. After a moment, he took one of the organist's oversized hands in both of his. "And us? I know. It's too soon. It was just one of those things. But I—I really *felt* something, Jim. I'm not surprised the earth moved.

Jim grinned shyly. "Good to know I haven't lost my touch, anyhow. And I'm not gonna say you're wrong, don't think that. But like you say, it is soon, and Katie needs me—heck, *I* need time to sort things out right now." Jim put his other hand over Braden's "You won't fret if we just sit back for a bit and see what the Lord has in store for us?"

Braden mustered a half smile. "No, Jim. I won't fret."

XXXVI WEAPON OF MASS CONSTRUCTION

On the strength of even larger profits from the 2003 Path to Judgment than the 2002 event had brought in, Pastor Long realized a decades-old dream with the purchase of the structure and trappings of a living Christmas tree. Naturally this weapon represented a significant escalation of the Jesus Wars. But for the moment that conflict had receded in popular consciousness, as a few rains after long drought, coupled with persistent, though so far minor tremors, had caused sinkholes to blossom all over town. Several vehicles, two sheds, at least one carport, and three family pets had been engulfed.

For the first time, more fingers than Delia's were pointing toward the quarry, but Harlan Stainsbury, StonyPoint Corporation's PR person, blandly insisted that while no one lamented these unfortunate occurrences more than the StonyPoint board, no evidence linked the company's operations to their mysterious causes.

The other wars had likewise receded. Security relaxed at workplaces. People stopped checking for white powder and mysterious packages in their mail, and President Bush gallantly flew over for Thanksgiving with the troops.

For all that, wars did go on, personally and nationally, internally and externally. Though Jim felt his heart was only a poor, rocky country, he resisted the brilliant flowering it did produce and grimly fought down the insurgency trying to protect such dangerous, opiate joy, so that his daughters might have a future and foreign invaders like Chase might take their nosy, destructive presence elsewhere.

For his part, Braden did his best to protect that same precious, exotic crop, but he, like the Taliban, found women getting in the way and invasive forces hunting him from pillar to post. Not only Jim's family, but Brenda's and his own mother, insisted on their right to rid him of all the "dangerous" impulses he harbored and impose their feminine, decadent ways on him.

Chase, meanwhile, felt himself attacked by rebellious emotional factions at every turn. Each step he took to satisfy or disguise his obsession seemed merely to start new threats and demons. He did not see or hear from Katie for the entire month of November, and this infuriated him. Finally, he gave up all pretensions to decency and resolved to get what he wanted by any means necessary. Only then, he believed, would peace be possible.

Even Christmas was an occasion for various pitched battles. At FBCJ there was the epic tree erection. Building the garland-covered pointy scaffold that would hold seventy people required a mighty effort akin to that exacted by the Egyptian pyramids it resembled. But if the Baptists recalled the Egyptians in enterprising industry, they were closer to the Greeks in disputatiousness, and indeed militarily the tree was to serve as a Trojan horse from which a mighty force would spring forth, subduing all resistance.

Unlike the Greeks, however, the Baptists harbored no doubts as to the wisdom and efficacy of their chosen tactic, but instead argued over their placement on the tree. "Don't think I don't know why John wants the tenors to go up on the third tier," Luraleen Whitfield confided to Sandra Briggs. "It's because Pastor Holloway put the sopranos on the bottom. John can look down into Krystal Wilcox' cleavage the whole time he's supposed to be singin' out the reason for the season. One of these days I'm just gonna straight up tell that woman to cover up." In the end, however, the age and conditioning of choir members were as much determining factors in their placement as anything else, with those who had vertigo, large girth, or weak legs taking spots on the lower tiers, and the younger and more able taking the higher.

Over at FUMC, Braden, feeling more and more like a subversive cell, persuaded Reverend Hollifield that the community needed a little innocent comic relief after so much war and trauma. With the carte blanche the kindly old man dispensed, he developed a program that featured, as a crowning hilarity, the ministers (with the more agile Leigh Ann Hollifield filling in for her Aunt Marian) reenacting the popular televised Christmas special from the previous year, *The Christmas Pixies*. Reverend Hollifield seemed positively delighted by his role as the evil Fairy Queen who tries to ruin Christmas by turning the pixies evil, but Cyrus, playing the role of the distressed little girl, Olivia, in a blond wig with two braids, was truly close to tears most of the time, and even though Craig Wright's role as a pixie gave him a chance to cavort with his fellow pixie, Leigh Ann, he was very tight-lipped about prancing around in tights, pointy ears, and an elf hat.

Yet there was nothing either of the junior ministers could say or do to stop it. Sometimes Braden positively hoped they would have it out with him so he could scream, "I'm gay, you morons," but whether from politeness or ignorance, no one ever did.

On Saturday, December 13th, both churches had had their respective Christmas concerts. As anyone following the Jesus Wars could have predicted, the majesty of the living Christmas tree crushed the light artillery of *The Christmas Pixies*, and the lesser male ministers at FUMC, excluding Braden, held a serious meeting with Reverend Hollifield in which they succeeded only in exacting a promise that their dignity and the church's would never again be compromised in such a manner. "At least it's *some*thing," Craig Wright sighed. But there seemed a danger that Braden's treachery, combined with Reverend Hollifield's lax oversight, could result in FBCJ becoming the dominant spiritual power in the troubled region of Jubilee.

#

After the pressures of the big Living Christmas Tree Program, Chase had a free day, and he knew exactly how he would employ it. Hannah Grace had told him that Katie was "*so* grounded" because her father had "like, gone ballistic" when he found out she had gone to "some college party," so Chase had taken to biking around, passing the Engels's house every hour or so, keeping watch. Around noon, everyone was still at home at Katie's house, so Chase headed downtown towards Henderson's BBQ for some ribs, fries, coleslaw, and iced tea. He spent a long time at Henderson's and riding around afterwards, trying to put down his personal insurgencies before once again giving up all hope of controlling them, except by realizing his one overriding dream of domination and relief. In that dream, Katie's tempting purity was to assuage his demons, but, he rationalized, her very sacrifice would be a saving, Christian act by which she would, if anything, only become more holy. He felt sure she would understand this and often wished he could explain it to her.

Back at Katie's house, his vigil was rewarded. Both cars were gone. Katie was on the porch reading a book and drinking a Coke. "Hey stranger," said Chase, slowing down and raising a hand.

"Pastor Moore!" Katie said. She dropped her book, jumped off the swing, and came to top of the porch steps with a smile that awakened a strong, unreasoning hope in Chase's heart. He stopped his bike and leaned on one leg irresolutely, still straddling the seat.

"Oh, come on up. Dad's practicing the organ, over at the church, Mom's at work, and I don't know where Lynette's got to. I know they won't let me see you, but they won't say why. Can you tell me?"

Chase dismounted. "T-to be honest with you, I haven't the slightest idea," he said. Leaning his bike against the porch steps, he sprang lightly up them. When he held out his arms, she flung herself into them. He hugged her as long as he could without arousing her suspicions. Her breasts were softer, more developed, even since last spring, but still small, and her shoulders still felt fragile and bony, and her honey-colored hair still smelled like lilacs. "Let's sit down," he said, gesturing toward the swing when at last he let her go.

They sat together, rocking gently. "This is all my fault," Katie said. "I hope you know I didn't just up and leave the church or anything like that."

"No—I didn't think that," Chase said, taking her hand.

She looked at him hopefully. "I still have my ring, you know. With her other hand, she drew the chain out from under her shirt and showed him.

"And I still have the k-key to your heart, Katie." He drew the key out of the pocket on his shirt and showed it to her. "I do still have it, really—d-don't I?" he asked, looking into her eyes.

They widened in alarm, but she reassured him. "Oh yes, Pastor Moore. I'm not perfect or anything—that's why Dad got so upset with me—but—"

"But you are still p-pure?" Chase interrupted, squeezing her hand without meaning to. She nodded rapidly. "Oh yes sir. I would never break a vow—you're kind of hurtin' my hand."

"Oh! Sorry," he said, letting go.

There was a pause. Suddenly Katie jumped up. "Where're my manners? You want a drink or something? Some Coke? Iced tea?"

"I guess I could use a C-Coke. Thanks," Chase said.

The whole thing was so easy. While she was getting it, he slipped a roofie into her Coke, and he even had time to get the water bottle filled with vodka that he had clipped to his bike and tip a little in—"for good measure," as he thought to himself, clipping the bottle back on.

She came back with a glass of Coke, and they swung for a while. "I'm so glad you stopped by," Katie said. "It's been so lonesome. Don't get me wrong—I don't exactly blame Dad for grounding me. I know I didn't act right, though for the life of me, I don't know how he ever found out. Maybe somebody at the gym. He goes over to the university gym a lot. You might as well know: I went to a frat party over there. But nothing bad happened like you talked about. Only I lied to my parents and told them I was sleeping over at Hannah Grace's."

She wasn't drinking, Chase noticed. "Well, he said, "that's pretty b-bad, but—let's drink t-to a fresh start."

She smiled and bent down to get her Coke. "I do think Dad'll let me come back to church soon. He said there were too many bad influences over there, but he's got to start trusting me again *some*time, doesn't he?"

"I'm sure he will," Chase said. "T-to a fresh start." They clicked their plastic glasses together and drank.

"I'm sorry you had to miss the Living C-Christmas Tree show," Chase said, moving to phase two of his plan.

"Oh me too," she said. "Hannah Grace called me up after the concert to tell me about it. I guess that was nice of her? It sorta seemed like she was almost happy she got to be in the show and I didn't."

"We c-could go over and see the t-tree now, if you want."

"Me and you together? Dad wouldn't like it. He says I'm not going anywhere till he says I can. Even though I've told him over and over again that I'm sorry and won't ever do it again."

"But K-Katie, I'm your pastor, not some frat b-boy."

"Yes, you are, and I trust you," Katie said dreamily, and she leaned her head experimentally on Chase's shoulder.

He felt unbearably tender toward her, and almost wished he had gone with his impulse to tell her everything and throw himself on her mercy. But no, this was safer. Get her to his office, have a few perfect hours with her, then after dark leave her on a bench in some park for the police to find. He had done some research. She wouldn't remember much, nor was anything traceable likely to show up in her blood by the time she was woke up or was found.

"I understand your father's concern," he said, "But I don't think it's g-good for you to stay away from ch-church. I'm not judging, b-but I just don't think JUMC is as serious about b-bein' saved an' all."

Katie took her head off his shoulder for another drink. "No they're not as serious, are they? Everyone says so." She jumped off the swing. "OK, let's go. Long as I can be back by four."

Chase looked at his watch. It was two thirty-four. "Sure. We c-can do that. Let's drink up."

XXXVII MORE EARTH-SHAKING REVELATION

He and Katie began walking toward the square, three blocks away. To Chase's dismay, there seemed to be a large gathering brewing there. Cars were parked on all the side streets, and many were still discharging passengers. Several people hailed Chase and Katie. But now that she had drunk the drug, Chase had no choice but to brazen it out. "Maybe this wasn't such a good idea," Katie said, uncertainly. "Someone might tell Dad they saw me out with you."

"And what's so wrong with th-that?" Chase said. He persuaded her that their best bet, with so much traffic coming into the square, was to head for the Family Life Wing and go to the sanctuary through there.

Katie nodded. "Maybe we better. I don't feel so good."

She was leaning on him as they entered the sanctuary. He would leave her behind the tree till he could be sure everyone had left the complex, then take her to his office. He wouldn't hurt her; she wouldn't know a thing about it.

"It's beautiful," she said, looking up at the towering red and gold tree. "Wish I could have been there . . . " Her voice trailed off, and she slumped against Chase as she collapsed.

Gently, he lifted her, carried her around behind the tree, and laid her down between its supporting uprights and two spiral staircases. She looked peaceful, and her face was white, almost translucent. Although it was December, the weather was unseasonably warm, and Katie was wearing only jeans and a thin, soft blue cardigan over a gray t-shirt that said "Peace on Earth" in red letters.

Chase hesitated to touch her. He knew he must keep his head and save all that for later, when no one was around. But he couldn't resist. He had to possess her purity to stop the demons, but he wouldn't hurt her. If only he could have explained it to her right, he was sure she would have wanted to help him. He moved his hand lightly over her hair, down her cheek, her neck, her sweater, over the softness of her breasts and the smooth expanse of her stomach. Then, lifting her toward him, he kissed her. One day he would tell her all about it, and she would understand.

Suddenly, he heard voices and lifted his head, paralyzed with fear. "Listen, Pastor, I can't tell you what this means. I just had no earthly idea this thing was gonna get so outa hand. The whole *town's* stirred up about it. I can't say as I blame 'em, but the traffic can't move through that mess at all, and honestly I'd be surprised if we got through it without anybody getting hurt. Now, we bring 'em—or at least most of 'em—in here, have 'em sit down, look at that beautiful tree—heck, they can't *help* lookin' at it—well, it'll just be a more *orderly* atmosphere. Everyone can have their say, if you see what I mean. Course, the city will pay any fees and whatnot."

"Not at all, Mr. Mayor. Happy to do it," came Pastor Long's soothing tones, and Chase could hear the minister's hand landing heavily on Mayor Grantwell's back.

"Thank you, Pastor. You have certainly relieved my mind."

#

Chase breathed easier as the crowd began to file in, making more than enough noise to mask anything coming from behind the tree. This meeting would not disturb his plans. Once everyone had gone home, there would still be plenty of time. He took Katie's head on his lap and began stroking her beautiful hair, idly listening to the speakers.

After everyone was settled, or at least had a spot to stand in, Pastor Long said it was his pleasure as Pastor of the First Baptist Church of Jubilee to host this important meeting to determine what measures the community should take in response to the sinkholes and seismic events that had literally shaken Jubilee to its core in recent weeks. He praised the wisdom of his friend, Mayor Grantwell, who, though he attended "that other church across the way," had chosen to move the meeting into FBCJ (this got some laughter; everyone knew FBCJ simply had the larger sanctuary). Finally, Pastor Long asked them to pray with him that God would guide them in their search for relief from their afflictions, whereupon all but Delia Rosenbaum bowed their heads.

After the prayer, the mayor thanked Pastor Long and politely introduced the city's consultant on the matter at hand, "Dr. Delia Rosenbaum." She took the microphone and began to explain about the sinkholes. She was very calm and reasonable, even when heckled and booed by the tougher characters in the crowd. She said things like, "As those of you who have a map or are close enough to mine up here can see, Jubilee is built over karst. Karst is simply limestone that over time has been eroded by water flowing through it underground." She explained how the quarry used a lot of water and showed the aquifers it had depleted and how when they were full they had supported the karst, but now that they were depleted, the whole town was resting on a lacy karst crust. She went on to explain how when rain washed silt into the cracks in the karst, stability was further compromised, the cracks widened, and sinkholes were liable to form.

Finally, she explained that the area was experiencing two types of tremors that further destabilized the karst. First, the quarry had recently increased the frequency and intensity of its blasting, as the table she had passed out showed. And second, the East Tennessee Seismic Zone, which extended well into Georgia, as they could see on the map, had recently become more active.

As she talked, the audience got quieter. Despite the dubious source, the information all seemed so reasonable, especially when Delia pointed to a spot over a depleted aquifer where a sinkhole had been documented and old Mrs. Farrow turned around proudly from her place in the front to announce, "That was on my farm," and added, her voice breaking, "Poor Pickles. He was only a kitten. Sucked him right in."

So now they listened quietly as Delia explained that she was in no way making any recommendation as to what course of action the town of Jubilee should take. Her role was only to acquire and relay pertinent information and data. And even though she lost much of the crowd with words like "pertinent," they accorded her a respectful hand as she stepped down from the altar area.

Next Mayor Grantwell introduced Harlan Stainsbury, who had come all the way from StonyPoint Quarry Company's Chattanooga office. Although an outsider, Stainsbury had an avuncular approach and delivery that seemed to go over well from the get-go. He expressed gratitude for the twenty-three-year partnership between his company and the town of Jubilee and concern for the sufferings of its citizens. He professed gratitude to "Mizz Rosenbaum" (who preferred to be referred to as "Doctor" or "Professor") for her "most interestin' charts and theories."

But, he explained, Mizz Rosenbaum had been rather narrowly focused on the quarry's role in depleting aquifers. In fact, almost all the aquifers in and around Jubilee were currently depleted. There were many causes for this too numerous and complex to go into at this time, but he would briefly sketch a few.

First and foremost, the drought had significantly lowered the water table. Then again, Jubilee's own growth, by paving over areas that had previously collected groundwater and increasing erosion and flash flooding, had prevented the replenishment of aquifers and increased the danger of silt washing into the karst that Mizz Rosenbaum had so helpfully pointed out. Finally, Jubilee's other industries, for instance agricultural irrigation, and even the lingering effects of the now defunct Braxton Dye Works, also helped to deplete aquifers. And he showed on a chart how aquifers in areas unlikely to be affected by the quarry were also depleted. Sadly, since no data on this phenomenon had been collected until the last ten years, and since the climate played such a large contributing role, it might never be possible to apportion blame for aquifer depletion with any degree of accuracy.

Turning to the matter of seismic tremors, Mr. Stainsbury again stated how grateful StonyPoint was to Mizz Rosenbaum for her detailed collection of data. By juxtaposing her chart of reported seismic occurrences with the quarry's blasting schedule, he explained, one could see that only a small fraction of the seismic events could conceivably be correlated to the quarry's schedule at all, and an even smaller number of those could possibly have the strength to cause tremors to be felt—faintly—as far as Jubilee. Those who had gotten a copy of the pie chart he had handed out or who were close enough to view the larger copy he had on the stage could see just how small a fraction of total occurrences could possibly be laid at StonyPoint's door.

Moreover, since the quarry operated exclusively beyond the official town boundaries, Mr. Stainsbury explained, it was beyond the legal jurisdiction of the town, which would have to pass whatever measures it saw fit to impose on its longtime partner and largest employer through the Butler County Commission.

Nevertheless, Mr. Stainsbury concluded, no one was more concerned about the wellbeing of the wonderful citizens of Jubilee than the board of StonyPoint Corporation, who had authorized him to make some very generous offers on their behalf. First, he had personally reviewed the rare incidences of tremors that had occurred in conjunction with blast activity at the quarry, and regardless of whether such conjunctions were coincidental or not, the blasting at those times would henceforth cease or be of significantly less force (healthy applause). Second, his company was committing some of its own top researchers in the areas of seismology, geology, and water resources to a full, five-year study of Jubilee's situation (less applause). Finally, he was authorized, if Mayor Grantwell and the council would permit, to make a generous gift as a gesture of goodwill from StonyPoint Quarry to its longtime friend and partner—a gift of fifteen *thousand* dollars for Munroe High's new Grantwell football field, henceforth to be called Grantwell-StonyPoint Field.

There was an eruption of cheering. Everyone had been looking forward to having a decent place for high-school football games since forever. Mayor Grantwell opened a side door, and Jenna Whitfield and another cheerleader, in full cheer dress, entered, smiling and carrying a huge check on which "To the city of JUBILEE, $15,000, FIFTEEN THOUSAND DOLLARS," was clearly visible.

Mayor Grantwell went up and shook hands with Mr. Stainsbury in front of the check, and the *Jubilee Sentinel* photographer ran up front to take their picture. "Thank goodness they'll be gone soon," thought Chase, behind the tree.

But just as the flash bulb went off, there was a resonant *Boom!* from under the floor, and the whole sanctuary seemed to shake. People screamed and started running for the door, but fortunately Officer Dillingham, who was up in the balcony, announced through his bullhorn, "Do not flee! I repeat: For your own safety, do not flee! Drop down and cover your head in case of falling debris. I repeat: Drop down and cover your heads!"

The disembodied voice froze many in their tracks. Only a very few careened outside. Most obediently crouched down and covered up. And so it was that much of the town witnessed the most momentous event in Jubilee since the Incident at its Junction.

First there was a tremendous lurch. The floor of the sanctuary seemed to sink beneath them. The stained-glass windows cracked, and two shattered, raining glass down on the crouching people below. Then, right up the center of the center aisle, a crack appeared. The carpet was torn apart, and through the crack in the concrete floor, those closest could see down to the remains of the fellowship hall, and below that a pit from which issued a cloud of dust and a terrible grinding noise.

Before they could recover from this, there was a cry from those nearest the tree, which had for some time been swaying back and forth as if trying to imitate a real tree. "Look out!" "She's gonna fall!" Jenna and the other cheerleader raced out the side door, and as many people as could make it followed. Others stumbled up the broken aisle, skirting the crack.

Fortunately the tree fell in very slow motion, and no one was seriously hurt. When it had crashed down, the sizeable crowd left in the sanctuary took a moment to notice a man covered with debris lying with a girl under him in his arms. Trying to escape with Katie in the confusion, Chase had been knocked unconscious by a falling piece of scaffolding.

Pulling off boards from the scaffolding and pieces of the boxes choir members had stood on to make them all the same height on the tree, people began to recognize the two figures. "Why that's Pastor Moore." "Who's the girl?" "That's Katie Engels, Jim and Judy's youngest." "Someone get a medic up here."

Long before the medics made it, though there were several in the crowd and the sirens were already wailing outside, Jim, who had come in looking for his daughter with a sinking feeling during Mr. Stainsbury's presentation, heard the cries and rushed up to the area where Chase and Katie lay. Over all the confusion his voice could clearly be heard. "What's *he* doing with *my* daughter?"

XXXVIII CONSEQUENCES

At the hospital it was discovered that Katie had Rohypnol in her blood, and although Chase at first denied having anything to do with that, enough people had seen him walking toward the church with her that he could not easily claim to have found her that way. In his hurry, Jim had not washed out the two glasses of Coke he had found on the porch, and so a clear chain of events was established.

Facing multiple serious charges and opprobrium from Jubilee to Atlanta (and even nationwide, among prurient internet users), Chase confessed and was sentenced to ten years in the Hardwater Penitentiary (not actually in that gentle community of Victorian homes, but some miles to the east), as well as to registry as a sex offender. He was barred from working with minors again, Omega Phi inflicted a post-graduation expulsion, and he was, of course, dismissed as youth pastor.

In his confession, Chase implicated Zach Finley, but since that heroic fellow had already volunteered and shipped out to Iraq, and since his mother had nursed the prosecutor, Charlie Nix, through his heart attack, and since the family was represented by the increasingly formidable Davis McGraw, Zach was given immunity, whereupon, via Skype, he fingered the fraternity, as the prosecutor, himself an Omega Phi man, had expected.

Fired with zeal to purge the site of his halcyon youth and supported by outraged public opinion, Prosecutor Nix descended like the wolf on the fold, launching a thorough investigation of Taylor, the fraternity, and even the lax oversight of the university itself. Fortunately for Omega Phi and the university, the fraternity president had acted on Chase's earlier warning, and no drugs of any kind were found on the premises. Taylor plea-bargained down to a misdemeanor and got five years, much of which was suspended, but he was expelled from both Omega Phi and NWGSU and never saw Jenna, who was already tiring of him, again. Omega Phi itself was suspended by the university for a full year.

Katie was sheltered from prying attention by her parents until after the Christmas break. When she did go back to school and church, she only frustrated the curious because she could really remember very little of the afternoon. Still, she was the subject of much finger pointing and speculation. Hannah Grace and Jenna agreed that she was getting very stuck up, especially since Jenna herself had very nearly met a similar fate, and so Katie's friendship with them ended.

#

For all intents and purposes, the Jesus Wars were over. At first it appeared that FBCJ had been utterly routed, its main building and its reputation both reduced to rubble in a single earth- shaking act of God (for it *was*, it transpired, a real earthquake, and not directly attributable to the quarry). But gradually, phoenix-like, it rose again.

First there was the feature in the *Weekly Inquirer* and *Weekly Inquirer Online* about Jubilee, the town whose quiet, law-abiding exterior masked the presence, known to all but unacknowledged, of a Satanic cult, complete with ritual virgin sacrifice. At a mass meeting of the cult, attended by the town's most eminent and highly respected citizens, including the mayor and a prominent Baptist minister, just as the ceremonial gang rape of the innocent virgin was about to commence, her father (who was present) was suddenly moved to object, and as he cried out to heaven, the earth trembled, the church split in two, and like the Philistines in their temple, all were killed, or at least maimed and taught a valuable lesson. Photos of Shelby Gilstrap in and around the church in full goth regalia were included to bolster the story's credibility, much to her amusement and her grandmother's shame.

Outrage over this libel brought the town together as one in support of FBCJ, and before long the congregation had built a brand-new church on the side of town farthest from the quarry, on inspected land and complete with safeguards built in by a firm from California that specialized in earthquake protection. They continued to produce Path to Judgment and the Living Christmas Tree Program annually. Indeed, their new sanctuary allowed for an even bigger tree, but whether because the new church was some distance from JUMC in the center of town, or because of the humbling ordeal the Baptists had passed through, a new spirit of isolationism arose between the two churches, and each was content to pursue its own religious identity again, with, for the most part, no thought of outdoing the other in anything.

#

Braden's departure also contributed to this new era, as his successor, though worthy, takes a more highbrow line with concerts. A number of factors were involved in Braden's decision to resign. First Jim, taken up with Katie and the inevitable press, resolutely declined to cultivate any relationship with him, and the specter of a similarly family-oriented future for himself drove Braden to leave all women behind and flee to a life of male companionship and struggle against the unfriendly forces seeking to capture him and force their all-American values down his throat.

Initially he had thought he might be able to give some ground but still remain an active force at JUMC. His mother, and especially Brenda, did not take his breaking the engagement well, but eventually his mother came around to the view that Brenda was really just not good enough for someone as talented as her son, and Brenda gave up calling and emailing. Some members of JUMC's staff and congregation may have speculated about his sexuality once the news was out about his break-up, but no one treated him differently to his face.

Still, as he prepared the third annual Fourth of July Celebration, Braden couldn't help feeling that the zest had gone out of his work. This was partly due to the nature of the 2004 celebration. The fighting was still raging overseas, and Jubilee had lost its first son, Private Dusty Mathers. Only a few weeks after hearing the news, his great-grandmother, old Mrs. Farrow, had died on her farm—of a broken heart, even the doctors admitted. Many other families were worrying and praying over sons and daughters serving in the military, and the death of much-beloved President Ronald Reagan on June 5th deepened the general gloom.

So this year's celebration was dedicated to military heroes. Gone was the Statue of Liberty, encouraged by Jesus-Marvin. There would be no stoking of righteous wrath from Alan Jackson, no self-glorifying patriotic pride stirred by Lee Greenwood or the Mormon Tabernacle Choir. Instead of Hackens's exultant *Te Deum*, JUMC would present a somber tribute to the fate of so many patriotic heroes. The men would sing "The Mansions of the Lord," Yolanda would bring back "Swing Low, Sweet Chariot," in addition to "The Battle Hymn of the Republic," Braden himself would sing "Wherever He Is Now" from the hit musical, *Soldiers*, and everyone would sing "The Star-Spangled Banner" earnestly at the end. Regretfully, Braden even gave up the confetti cannon.

On the other hand, he demonstrated his great showmanship when he invited Dusty's mother, Ruth Farrow Mathers, to the concert. She was a shy, thin widow with light brown hair like Dusty's, thick glasses, and clumsy, sun-browned hands that she didn't seem to know what to do with since his funeral. Ruth had lived most of her life on the farm with old Mrs. Farrow, which wasn't always easy, and she only came into town when she absolutely had to. She still remembered how the town girls had made fun of her homemade clothes and refusal to dance at a Baptist youth conference many years ago.

Nevertheless, when Braden explained that the concert was to honor Dusty's memory and pay tribute to our military, she came and marveled at the lights, the costumes, the orchestra. She sat in the front pew, stood when introduced, sat down again, and, folding her unruly hands, numbly let it all wash over her.

On the whole she felt she had played her part well when it was done. The only really hard times were when that Yolanda Tibbets had brought over those lilies to her after "The Battle Hymn of the Republic," the *Soldiers* song, and towards the end of "The Mansions of the Lord," when the men sang, "Where no mothers cry / and no children weep. . . ." She knew that no mothers were crying because it was heaven, but it still made her feel as if Dusty had gone to a cold bleak place far away from her.

The "Tribute to the Armed Forces" helped perk her up again, though. Overall she reckoned it was nice, and she knew everyone meant to be kind.

XXXIX ENDINGS AND BEGINNINGS

Everybody else who was at the Celebration, which was everyone who could squeeze into the church, congratulated Braden on the appropriateness of the concert in these troubled times, the moving power of his solo, and the wonderful way he had honored Dusty's memory and Mrs. Mathers. But Braden himself felt strangely empty. He kept remembering the kiss and its frustrating promise that had never been fulfilled, though of course Jim had been very kind and sorry about that. Suddenly, Braden realized he was lonely. He missed Brenda—if only she hadn't come with so many strings attached—but even more he missed what he and Jim should have had.

So one day he went to talk to Reverend Hollifield, who seemed stricken but said Braden must go where the Lord led him.

Half an hour later, Braden was crying into his ribs at Henderson's BBQ. Where would he go? What would he do? He became aware that a heavy body had deposited itself opposite him. Lifting his head, he found it was Yolanda.

She leaned across the table. "Mr. Braden! Get ahold of yourself. This here's bad for business! Look, I got you a to-go box here. Let's put those ribs in there, pop 'em in this here bag, and then you come in the back for a little heart-to-heart."

On the short walk to her office, Braden tried to pull himself together. "I've just quit my job at the church, you see," he said, as he sat down across from her, just as he had on his first office visit, so long ago. "I know that probly comes as a surprise to you—I don't know how to explain it—"

"Hmm," said Yolanda. "It couldn't be because you're gay?"

Braden gaped. "But how did you—?"

"Huh," said Yolanda. "I wasn't born yesterday."

"Do you—disapprove? It's against your religion, isn't it?"

"Honey, just 'cause I go to the church don't mean I let the preacher tell me how to think. To me, religion is just Jesus. It's just about loving each other and all that kinda good stuff."

"That's exactly what I believe too, Yolanda. But it sure is nice to hear someone say it right now." Braden found he really did feel better.

As if to make up for her lapse into sentiment, Yolanda became all business. "Now listen to me. You got to get to Hot-lanta, boy. It's the only way. But tell the truth now: how do you feel about my people? Working with us, I mean."

A film of every real and virtual encounter he'd ever had with black people ran in Braden's head at top speed, but it was too various to be of much help. "I—I don't know," he said. "I don't think I'd mind working with African Americans."

"Good," said Yolanda. "Then I can help you. This"—she pushed a business card across the table—is Henderson Barbecue's new flagship restaurant, set to open next month in Buckhead. Now there's always a server's job for you there if you're desperate.

"But mostly I just expect you to eat there and bring all your friends, because *this* is my cousin, Debra Bradshaw's, card. Debra's a real go-getter, like me, and she has just founded the first fully accredited, all-black prep school in the Atlanta metro area. Not that she discriminates in admissions, or anything, but the school just happens to be in a certain part of Dekalb County where the million-dollar homes are one hundred percent black-owned."

Yolanda paused proudly to enjoy Braden's surprised look. He had not thought of himself as racist, but this Alice in Wonderland image had not been in his film. "Anyway," Yolanda went on, "I happen to know they are looking for someone who can do what you do—you know, show choir, musicals, that king of thing. If you're interested, I'll shoot Debra an email tonight."

"Thank you," Braden said, humbly. "I really can't thank you enough."

"Just don't program no 'Dixie,' now," Yolanda said, with a wink. As Braden was leaving, she added, "And heat up those ribs good before you eat 'em. I put some extra sauce packets in for you. You can pay your ticket up at the register."

#

Every Saturday when the weather is fine (except in October, when his plane is commandeered for Path to Judgment), Sam Braxton leaves his restaurant in the hands of a family member and takes off. Sometimes he goes to a football game, or to his cousin's horse farm in Tennessee, or to look over some Civil War battlefield. The destination is not as important to him as the flight itself. Like Jordan Gilstrap, looking down on the inhabitants of Jubilee from the vantage point of her illustrious ancestor, Sam finds a certain peace in a change of perspective. Rising higher and higher into the sky, he watches the populace and their myriad concerns shrink to insignificance, then leaves them behind altogether. He no longer worries about the latest meeting of the Braxton Foundation, or about his wife, off shopping for expensive designer items in Atlanta, or about whether his children will keep the restaurant going when he retires. He is in flight and, for a time, free.

Just so, we must now leave Jubilee and its concerns behind. But before they quite disappear from view, we will take note of some of our more particular friends and acquaintances and how they have fared in the decade since the Jesus Wars came to an end.

To no one's surprise, Pastor Long eventually received a call to one of the large Baptist churches in Atlanta, where he and his wife are very happy and have won many souls for the Lord. Jeff Randle briefly succeeded Pastor Long before becoming the chaplain at NWGSU. The Longs' great friend, Patricia Honeywell, continues to pen works of Christian fantasy. When sales fell off during the Great Recession, she began a new series, "Angels vs. Demons," that includes horror. It has done very well.

Braden of course made good in Atlanta, and though he was very happy at Debra Bradshaw's W. E. B. DuBois Academy, he soon made the transition to Atlanta's theater scene, where he is a sought-after musical director and not at all lonely. He remains a devout Methodist, and his mother has become an enthusiastic member of PFLAG. They frequently dine together at Henderson's BBQ in Buckhead, and there they often encounter Yolanda, who relocated after Artie's retirement from the NWGSU coaching staff. He enjoys gardening and helping out the Dubois Academy football team.

Though her company is much in demand to set off more attractive female friends, Brenda takes solace mostly in her cats and the children she teaches at Jefferson Davis Elementary in Noble. She tries to work out and attends the singles group at the First Methodist Church of Noble religiously.

Izzy Henderson passed away in 2005, but Althea Abbott Henderson lived long enough to see her son Johnny become a congressional representative. He is happy in his work, as is his great friend, Bishop (formerly Pastor) Thornberry in his.

Jim Engels is a devoted family man, and if he is often lonely and occasionally unfaithful, nobody knows anything about it. Lynette is getting a doctorate in music education from the University of Miami, where her husband is a straight pianist on the faculty. Katie grew up to be quiet, studious, and a serious Methodist. When representatives of various true crime shows came calling after the *Inquirer* story, Jim and his family finally decided to sell Katie's story, provided the family's names were changed. This generated a tidy sum that helped pay for her to go to Emory University, where she is now doing graduate work in psychology.

In her senior year of high school, Jenna Whitfield was crowned Quarry Queen. She went on to get a degree in early childhood education at NWGSU, but married a wealthy lawyer soon after and is now climbing to the top of the Hardwater social ladder. Chuck Whitfield lost his leg in Iraq, but does well with his prosthesis. If he keeps up with his A.A. meetings, the family is hopeful he may one day take over His Word, which continues to prosper.

Reverend Hollifield has retired and lives with his wife in Jubilee's Live Oaks Plantation assisted living facility. Cyrus Buell succeeded him at JUMC, and although he lacks his predecessor's erudition, he is highly regarded for his sensitivity and kind heart.

Rita and Marvin Patterson are still together; Ron Wylie is still single and happy-go-lucky; May Ewing still tyrannizes over the bell choir, which has won several awards. Macy Munroe has just finished homeschooling Tyler. Her older children are all successful, and her eldest daughter is a fashion designer in Atlanta where, despite daily rubbing shoulders with "different" people, she remains strong in her faith. Lydie has passed on, as has poor Miss Sarah Jo, bless her heart. She and her iced tea are sorely missed at meetings of Jubilee's chapter of the Daughters of the Confederacy.

As I mentioned, Jordan Gilstrap was mentored by Delia Rosenbaum at NWGSU, where Jordan set several athletic records. After her graduation, she and Delia became committed partners and were wed as soon as Georgia law permitted. Delia has gone into consulting full-time, and Jordan is her assistant. She holds a master's degree in geology from the University of Georgia and has converted to reformed Judaism, to which Delia has returned.

Upon her release with a clean record from the Butler County Girls Ranch, where she was sent after a misunderstanding over a car she borrowed, Shelby Gilstrap was encouraged by tough love from her sister to get her GED, after which she learned welding at Butler Community College. It so happened that Zach Finley, honorably discharged with a Silver Star, was also pursuing an interest in welding. The two fell in love and eventually married. Their furniture made out of welded, found materials is available for purchase at their studio out in the county and at several pricey Atlanta boutiques. Zach sometimes gets together with buddies to play music, but since his return from Iraq he prefers a calmer life. He and Shelby do not attend church. Zach believes, but Shelby is agnostic.

Ruby Gilstrap passed on a few years ago. She remained a Baptist till the end, but never let her faith come between her and her granddaughters.

The Dillinghams have experienced the most striking change in their fortunes. Not surprisingly, Jacob Dillingham's meteoric rise to Chief of the Jubilee Police Department dates from his alert response to the earthquake that destroyed FBCJ, for which he was commended and awarded a medal. But that day had consequences for Rachel Dillingham as well. During the making of the true-crime story of Chase and Katie, she was interviewed in the hope that, as Chase's half-sister, she could perhaps shed light on his motivation. In an attempt to help her brother, she explained how, while her stepfather was molesting her after he lost his job and took to drink when the mill closed, he used to make Chase, who was five at the time, keep watch outside. She said she didn't know if Chase knew what he was doing then, or if he even remembered it, since the family never talked about it.

This tale did conjure up sympathy for Chase, heretofore a pariah, and Pastor Long made him a special object of care in FBCJ's prison ministry. Partly with this help and partly on the strength of his own fruitful ministerial work in prison, Chase found a job after his release helping ex-cons find their footing in the outside world. Every summer, Chase leads a group of them in a retreat in the North Georgia Mountains. The men sit around the fire and sing songs, their faces shining and a love for Jesus in their hearts.

But Rachel's interview had an even greater effect on her own life. She wrote up an account of her past and the recent events in Jubilee that was snapped up by a publisher and eventually turned into the Lifetime movie, *Wounded Innocence.* Fired up, she researched other true crime stories, and options on several of her books were bought by Hollywood studios.

Bewildered and not entirely pleased by his wife's career, Jake Dillingham allowed her to slip away. After the divorce was final, she moved the family to California, where she is a writer and motivational speaker. She still considers herself a Baptist, but rarely has the time to attend church. T. J. is a freshman at Berkeley majoring in integrative biology and minoring in philosophy. He is not sure what he believes, but he wants to save endangered species, and he likes phenomenology. Hannah Grace attended USC but dropped out to pursue acting full-time. She can be seen in the remake of *House of Gore*, where she plays screaming girl number four, and in a commercial for Sheen shampoo. She is Facebook friends with Jenna and still considers herself a Baptist, though she is drawn to Scientology.

Finally, StonyPoint Quarry continues to operate outside Jubilee. Thanks to the unlikely team of Delia Rosenbaum and Davis McGraw, several citizens in and around the town have received sizeable settlements, including Ruth Mathers, who inherited the farm with the sinkhole that swallowed up Pickles, and the whole town enjoys the Grantwell-StonyPoint Football Field. Drought conditions have let up for now, mitigating the sinkhole problem, the quarry is monitoring its blasting more carefully, and the East Tennessee Seismic Zone has been quiet of late.

#

So now, friends, as Pastor Long says at the end of his weddings, you are dismissed. May your flight be safe and your reception, wherever you land, long on delights and short on speeches.

THE END

ABOUT THE AUTHOR

Lorna Wood lives, writes, and plays music in Auburn, Alabama. She has published stories, poetry, and essays, and the novella, *Family Values*. When not writing, teaching, or practicing, she enjoys spending time with her grown children, her husband, and her cat.

www.ingramcontent.com/pod-product-compliance
Ingram Content Group UK Ltd.
Pitfield, Milton Keynes, MK11 3LW, UK
UKHW022021190726
13853UKWH00005B/2043

9 798709 745674